March 2020

To my very
John,
In memory of a
special friendship,
love, always
Wendy.

HUGILL'S MESSAGE

WENDY MILLS

Produced in United Kingdom

Cover Design and Layout by SpiffingCovers

For Sarah, Sam, James and Edie

This story was written in gratitude to Charles Darwin, for his Tree of Life ('On the Origin of Species') and for having discovered our place in it.

ACHNOWLEDGEMENTS

Sometime in the summer of 1986 Marje Sherman and I were standing at Leicester Square Underground (on the Piccadilly Line) with our families when we saw mice scurrying under the rails. She suggested I write a story about them.

I completed Hugill's Message in late 1987. I would like to thank those who helped in varying ways at the time: Marje for that gentle nudge, my dearest parents, Cherry and Roger Fisher, for their enthusiasm and editorial advice, Rodney Douglas and Lauriston Kellaway for your creative suggestions with aspects of the text, and Maggie Kay for your beautiful illustrations. Hugill's Message was always going to have a hard time coming into the world because it was so difficult to categorise, aimed as it was for children and for the child in all adults. So I put the manuscript away.

In 2010 my husband and I went to Kenya. Thank you Bastone Shitandi for taking us on an amazing journey through Central Kenya and for your own insights into the animal world you grew up with, enabling me to improve my text.

And my treasured daughter Sarah Douglas and dear Carol Schonauer, bless you always for your constant faith in me and my story over years and years.

My heartfelt thanks to everyone at SpiffingCovers for your meticulous guidance, creative enthusiasm and skills, and your kindness. Always approachable and sensitive, Hugill's Message and my beloved animal characters had indeed found the right home at last. Well worth the wait!

Finally, none of this would have been possible without the support of my dearest Chris. Thank you forever.

‘we can understand how it is that all forms of
life, ancient and recent, make together one grand
system; for all are connected by generation.’

Charles Darwin: *‘On the Origin of Species.’*

CHAPTER ONE
A VOICE FROM THE PAST

If the great occurrence from the sky had not happened on that particular day and just at that moment then, I, Livingstone of Leicester Square Underground, archivist and keeper of the records of the family, would not have ventured so far with Grandfather Darwin and this tale would never have been told. But it did happen and the Great African Adventure is perhaps one of the most extraordinary stories in our family annals.

It all began when Grandfather Darwin and I were sitting on the top step of Piccadilly Circus sharing a hot, fire-browned chestnut. A light snow wafted towards us out of a leaden sky. It was decidedly not the day for an adventure. So we sat together in a contented huddle, keeping each other warm and watching the great world as it milled and muddled about us.

I was very busy working my way through a juicy hole in my end of the chestnut when I became aware that Grandfather was absorbed in the sky. I turned my attention away from the nut, from feet scrunching on wet tar and the strident sounds of hooters and brakes and followed his gaze. At first I could see nothing. And then, through the snow, I discerned a brown-black flying object coming slowly towards us. Like some fearsome apparition it emerged from the endless grey background, to draw near and to hover ominously. I realized then that it was a huge brown bird... a bird with a grand white chest and an extensive brown wingspan! It descended gradually until it flew over Piccadilly, its brown head bent downwards and moving rapidly this way and that, first watching the streets and then the steps, and then back to the streets again, frantically searching for something, or so it seemed to me. Then it made repeated dives towards the steps, where it looked around urgently before it climbed up high again to resume its circling. This ungainly activity continued for quite some time.

Grandfather put up his binoculars to get a better look. At length I asked him what kind of bird it could possibly be, to have been attracted to the cold and wintry North. 'I do believe…if I'm not mistaken, Livingstone, that it's a Martial Eagle, from East Africa. Now what can he be doing here I wonder?'

The eagle was now directly above us, phantom-like with his wings outstretched. Then he seemed to come to a decision because he suddenly swooped down and landed a few paces away, where he stood very stiffly, his piercing yellow eyes staring straight ahead.

Overcome with curiosity, Grandfather sidled up to the old bird. 'Rather a strange time of year to be visiting Piccadilly, or are you perhaps lost?' he asked politely.

The eagle didn't answer but gazed deeply into Grandfather's eyes. Then he sighed hopelessly and said: 'Am I addressing Grandfather Darwin Mouse of Leicester Square Underground by any vague chance?'

'You most certainly are,' cried a surprised Grandfather, 'at your service!' he continued with a little bow.

'Oh! Do you think so? I mean, I do hope so,' replied the eagle dolefully. Then he sniffed and turned his brown, craggy old face slightly away from us. He shook his wings, his whole body, lifted each talon and puffed out his chest: 'The name's Warrior.' An unfathomable silence followed. We waited uncomfortably, scuffling our paws. 'I've brought a message…from an old friend,' he continued finally, and turned again to gaze intently into Grandfather's eyes.

Grandfather in his turn gazed silently back, not wishing to upset the old bird by urging him to speak.

The eagle was suddenly gripped by some deep emotion, his whole body shook and his talons rattled alarmingly on the stone. 'Your friend saved my life many years ago…' he said, turning away, as if to banish the memory, 'so you see, I had to come…to help out.' The speech seemed to exhaust him completely and he shut his eyes tucking one leg under his wing and sighing deeply.

We waited politely. The minutes ticked by. When nothing further seemed forthcoming we walked around the old bird.

'What should we do?' I whispered to Grandfather.

'Well, let's see…perhaps the message is tucked away somewhere.'

We crept closer and peeped in under his wings.

'Africa!' cried the eagle, waking suddenly and wobbling dangerously on his one leg. We quickly stepped back and waited. 'Alas! I sleep such a lot these days,' he sighed and a large tear rolled to the tip of his rather yellowed, cracked beak.

'Er…you said something about Africa,' said Grandfather a little brusquely.

'Africa? Did I really? How odd! Perhaps I was dreaming? Alas…I dream such a lot these days too…' and he sniffed and turned away.

By now Grandfather was becoming rather impatient. Piccadilly steps in the middle of winter with a light snow falling was hardly the place to wait for a mysterious message that wouldn't come. 'My dear Sir,' he said, 'you told us you had a message from an old friend of mine.'

'Oh yes…so I did…but that's why I'm here!' replied the eagle, suddenly becoming angry and snapping his beak, quite as if we had been responsible for keeping him waiting all this time. 'Now what was it? Hmmm…let me think. Oh yes, this is the message:

Come to Africa, to Kenya. Have stumbled on something. A great story to be told.

'Are you sure there was nothing more?' asked Grandfather.

'I wouldn't have been able to remember more. It took all my energy making this long journey,' replied the eagle, flapping his wings and preparing for a lift-off. 'Oh dear, I must go, I can't bear snow,' and with that he slowly launched himself into the grey, his wingtip grazing the top of Eros slightly.

'But who's it from?' cried Grandfather.

The departing eagle looked sadly back at us as he turned to head South. 'Hugill Macauley,' came the ghostly, wind-borne reply.

'Hugill Macauley!' breathed Grandfather, gazing in the direction of the eagle, now a black dot in the sky. He sat down heavily on the top step. 'Can it possibly be, after all these years?'

'Who is he Grandfather?' I asked.

No reply came. Instead Grandfather began to laugh and then he grabbed the end of his tail, giving it an excited kiss. 'We're going to Africa, Livingstone! We're going to Africa!' and he bounded down the steps and hurried in the direction of our home on the Underground.

'Hugill Macauley needs me, Columbus! Amelia!' announced Grandfather loudly as he pushed open our front door.

'Oh!' said father, looking up from mounds of papers and accounts. 'Where's he this time?'

'East Africa…Kenya. He has cousins out there. Anyway, can I take Livingstone? It's time he had a look at Africa.'

Father and mother looked at each other and then at me waiting expectantly at the door. 'Why not!' said father.

'But do promise to bring him back with you Darwin,' said mother.

And that was that.

Of course, preparing for a trip to Africa proved to be no easy task. Grandfather briefed me on the importance of 'travelling light.' But mother kept slipping in extra vests and pairs of shoelaces and father pressed socks onto me, saying that that was the item he missed most on his last big adventure. In no time at all the two were arguing about the relative merits of extra pairs of shoelaces over extra pairs of socks, with Grandfather hopping about us whispering 'don't take any,' 'don't take any,' and no matter how often I packed and repacked my rucksack, it always seemed to bulge in all sorts of odd places. At last I sorted out my clothing to the satisfaction of all three experienced adventurers, leaving a large pile of odds and ends on the floor by the fire. I was travelling light, but only just.

The more important items came next: one compass, lovingly cleaned and polished by father on our behalf; a torch; all of Grandfather's old maps of East Africa; a medical kit consisting of snake-bite antidotes, malaria pills and sunburn cream; a water bottle each; a long piece of climbing rope; a tin box of rations for each of us containing Grandfather's special restorative dry wholemeal biscuits made from a secret recipe given him by a mouse who kept getting lost in the Urals; a small tin of sardines, sugar, chocolate and wind dried sausage; last of all Grandfather's binoculars and my beloved magnifying glass, without which items no adventure could ever be possible. We were packed and ready to go!

It was nightfall. One by one we ascended the platform to await the Heathrow-bound train. With tears in her eyes, mother handed Grandfather a tablecloth rolled around some warm bread and delicious smelling cheese. 'For the road,' she whispered, kissing him lightly between the eyes. And then she clasped me firmly to her chest, and in a hoarse voice said: 'Do be careful…be sure to stick close to Grandfather.' Father shook hands with Grandfather and squeezed me roughly to him. 'Bon Voyage,' he mumbled shyly and we hopped into the train. We scuttled between the passengers' feet to a dark spot under one of the chairs and settled ourselves down comfortably, close to the rattle of wheels and warmed by the dull throbbing of the carriage floor. The first leg of our long journey had begun.

CHAPTER TWO

GRANDFATHER DARWIN TELLS A STORY

'If I know Hugill Macauley there's a lot more of his message still to come, and the unfolding of it will be very complicated indeed,' said Grandfather, neatly placing two thick slices of cheese on a chunk of warm bread.

'Why is that Grandfather?' I asked.

'Hugill Macauley works in mysterious and wizardly ways…it's his background you know,' and he took a large bite of bread and cheese.

'But who is he? Tell me his story.'

Grandfather munched deliberately and gazed silently at a colourful pair of shoelaces across the aisle. Then he swallowed and sighed: 'Hugill Macauley's story…mmm… now there's a tale worth the telling and if I'm not mistaken, it will take as long as our long journey to Africa. To begin at the beginning of Hugill's strange life is to begin in a circus caravan one freezing cold night in Moscow…'

I nestled closer and waited for more.

'According to his mother, whom I met quite by chance in a fairground in Ireland, he made a great noise when he came into the world. It disturbed the lions and elephants in particular; they became restless and moaned and thrashed against the bars of their cages. It reminded them too much of Africa, of home, that noise of an animal being born, even though he was only a monkey and not one of their own kind.'

'A monkey!' I interrupted.

'Oh! Didn't I tell you that Hugill Macauley is a monkey? Gha!...gha!...gha!' he laughed gruffly, throwing his head back and scattering bread crumbs all over me. 'Well then, I must go back a bit. Hugill Macauley comes from a long line of European organ grinders and entertainers extraordinary: magicians, musicians, clowns, acrobats, trapeze artists, fortune-tellers...there was nothing that that travelling monkey troupe did not try throughout their travels across Europe from London to Moscow and back. His father came from a famous English family of organ grinders on the one side and a renowned Scottish family of magicians on the other. His mother came from a long line of French acrobats and Russian fortune-tellers.

'But to go back to Hugill's own beginnings. His parents were delighted when he was born. He was their first son after seven daughters! In other respects his birth came at a bad time in the history of the family, because that same evening the owner of the circus had announced that the circus was closing. It was wartime in Europe and too few had money or inclination to attend circuses. The larger animals were to be shipped off to the South of Italy for safety and the monkeys were free to leave. The Macauley family had only three days to pack their belongings and depart the circus for ever.

'Hugill clung to his mother as the entire Macauley troupe, including cousins, aunts and uncles from the Russian, French, English and Scottish sides of the family, set off West, towards France. In tow, of course, was the beloved family organ, which Hugill's father began teaching him when he was only a week old. And that, my dear Livingstone, remains his most pleasurable memory from those dark days. Ahh…and they were indeed very bleak: travelling through a war-torn and poverty stricken Europe; entertaining in dingy, ill-lit inns or in cold, windswept cobbled squares; hiding in shelters, in farm haylofts and trees; scratching about for food but starving most of the time; and the cold…the cold…it always seemed to be winter. It was a bad time for all animals…so little food, so much danger. Hugill doesn't like speaking about those early years. I wouldn't refer to them if I were you. He'd probably evade your questions; slide out of it by doing a somersault, or hiding behind a juggling act.

'After the war he parted from his family, preferring to travel the world alone, his beloved organ on his back. He travelled to North Africa, to the Far East, throughout Europe, even South America. When he was in his late twenties he joined a large circus in Spain where he met a young Indian elephant named Fayum the Third. They soon became close friends, and Hugill invented an extraordinary juggling act on Fayum's back which never ceased to delight the crowds.

'One day, while they were practising in the ring, Hugill noticed that Fayum seemed indifferent, even apathetic.

"What's wrong my friend?" he asked the elephant.

Fayum remained silent, just curling and uncurling his trunk as he tramped around the ring.

"It's no good Fayum," Hugill said, "there's no point in us continuing unless you tell me what the matter is."

'Fayum dejectedly carried Hugill out of the tent and to a private part of the fairground. In the shade of an old tree, he told Hugill how he had been kidnapped from his mother's side when only a year old and sold to a circus in Delhi. There he lived on the edge of starvation until he was bought by another circus and shipped to Italy. He was sold twice more until he and Hugill met. "Hugill my friend, my only friend," said the young elephant heavily. "I can't perform another trick…I've had enough. I want to go home…to my family." A silence followed, broken only by the leaves whispering above them. Fayum moved heavily from one foot to another while he awaited Hugill's reply.

'Meanwhile, Hugill somersaulted into the tree and leapt to its topmost branches. There he sat thinking very deeply, his head cocked to one side, and pulling gently at his monkey-beard. At last, when Fayum was about to trumpet out loud with impatience, Hugill descended rapidly through the tree and landed with a bump on the elephant's back…Oh dear, Livingstone…the train has arrived, my story will have to wait! Quick! Roll up the bread and cheese, we have to hurry!'

So deeply absorbed was I in Grandfather's tale that I hadn't even noticed the train come into our station. Exotic images of circus tents, lions, elephants and monkey troupes were hastily cast aside. I grabbed the bread and cheese and chased after Grandfather's tail as it disappeared through the train door.

Years of adventure and exploration have taught the Leicester Square Mice, Grandfather in particular, just how to find their way around Heathrow and what kind of hand luggage to hide in. To that end we made our way to the departure lounge for the Kenyan flight and saw just the right bag, of a dull ochre leather and with lots of soft, spacious side-pockets. We slipped into a pocket unnoticed and awaited our turn to enter the plane.

Once inside we leapt out of the pocket and ventured across the cabin to a choice spot known only to Grandfather and to those who had ever had the privilege of travelling with him: a thickly carpeted dark corner to the left of the kitchen. Thus situated, we were ensured of a continuous supply of excellent food throughout the journey.

'Now where was I?' Grandfather asked, his eyes mesmerised by a mouth-watering square of cheese disappearing into my mouth.

'Hugill's plan,' I replied.

'Oh yes. Well, he landed on Fayum's back saying with a characteristic shrug: "And so you shall go home… and so you shall. We'll finish our act tonight and when we walk out of the tent, we won't stop, we'll simply carry on walking." And that's exactly what they did. That night they gave their last and finest performance, and then they circled the ring three times, bowing deeply to the frenzied clapping and loud whistles, and left the tent through the large flap at the back. They stopped at Hugill's caravan to fetch his beloved organ and some provisions and set off on their long journey, looking neither left nor right and behaving as if they were just going out for an evening stroll.

'They walked for many weeks: through thickets and forests, along rivers and beside lakes; over hills and through steep, craggy mountain passes. They kept to the wilder parts of each country through which they walked, travelling mainly at night. Their only companions on this unusual journey were the wild animals: deer, badgers, wild pigs, birds, field mice, foxes, otters and many, many more. Later on, when they got deeper into Afghanistan and then Pakistan, they came across snakes of every description and even tigers. Each encounter was always accompanied by the usual animal inquisitiveness: "What's your story? Where are you going?" And when Hugill and Fayum had told their tale, they were in turn regaled with stories from their newfound friends, and, of course, advice on delicious berries and fruits; hidden dangers and directions.

'They became so well-known that their story was passed on ahead of them. By the time they reached the borders of North-Western India, they had an inkling that they were already expected. Even the wind seemed to whisper: "It's the circus friends…it's the circus friends… they've come at last…at last…at last…" A multitude of birds hovered in trees to peep at them through leaves and branches. They were surrounded by yellow eyes darting here and there, shyly staring, yet deeply hidden by lattice-like foliage. On and on they walked through the wild forests and jungles of the Punjab. By now Fayum was light of step; his trunk arched joyously, pulling at a leaf overhead, darting to tickle a furry body below, curling round his big bulbous form to give his dear friend Hugill a squeeze. At every new glimpse of the horizon he would flap his ears and trumpet: a wild, high-pitched yell which echoed through the forest, bouncing off trees and rocks. And amidst such a clear demonstration of happiness, Hugill began to grind his organ, something he only did on rare and special occasions. Its haunting melodious European notes contrasted oddly with the wilder notes of the Indian jungle. So, this whimsical strangely matched pair crashed their animated and noisy way through the trees.

'It was when they had entered a particularly dense part of the forest that they were treated to quite a different jungle sound in response to their music. It came from above, an avalanche of words that fell wildly about them amidst loud shrieks and screams and laughs.

"What a cacophony! What a cacophony! Call it off! Call it off! We've had enough! We've had enough! Are you the circus pair? What took you so long? Why have you got an organ? How noisy…hahaha…how silly. No!No!No! Not that way, there's too much creeper there, try this path. Come on…hurry up!"

'Fayum squeaked to silence and stopped dead in his tracks. Hugill's organ playing ground to a halt, the notes floating away into the green gloom. The two animals looked around them in silence. Who could it be?

'The voice came again: "Follow me! Follow me! Me! Me!"

"Follow who?" asked Hugill.

"Me!" screamed the voice.

'They looked up into the trees. And there, sitting on a branch above them, was a bright luminous green parrot with red-tipped wings, a yellow beak and red-rimmed eyes.

"Who is me?" asked Fayum.

"Me is myself, myself I am and I am me and Kush is my name and follow me! me! me!" replied the parrot in frustration, all the while hopping and bobbing and moving restlessly up and down the branch.

'Hugill and Fayum did as they were told. They could hardly refuse this flying torrent of words, since they were sure that any rebellion on their part would be treated with squawks and repetitions. So they followed Kush through the jungle. It was a most circuitous route; twice round large trees, backwards round rocks and through deep tunnels of intertwined branches and leaves. And throughout the parrot prattled continually, asking questions about their journey and never waiting for a reply; discussing the weather, laughing uproariously now and then at the surprise in store for the strange pair.

'Suddenly the jungle seemed to thin out and they burst their way into a huge circular clearing. It was filled with elephants moving heavily against one another, trunks swinging and feet stamping. Fayum, with Hugill on his back and Kush on his head, moved to the centre of the ring. He turned round slowly, gazing in silent awe at the immense army of elephants about him. They all trumpeted loudly and shuffled closer together to make an opening. And through it came an old hugely tusked elephant. He loomed over Fayum, the tip of his trunk moving rapidly over the younger elephant's body. When this curious ritual appeared to be over he trumpeted:

"Welcome!"

'The word echoed through the jungle, slipping through the trees and falling down the rivers, to be heard with a mysterious softness from far away. "I am your Grandfather, Fayum the First. At last you have returned to take your rightful place at my side," continued the great elephant leader.

'Fayum bowed his head in deference. He moved closer and rubbed his younger, softer body against the thick old hide. "It has been many years," he whispered. "And the burden has been very great."

'The old elephant flapped his huge scarred ears and trumpeted softly in reply.

"But where are my parents?" asked Fayum, looking at the surrounding group.

"Alas," sighed his grandfather, so heavily that dust and dry grass flew up around them in a golden haze, "they perished in the flood that came with the great monsoon of many wet seasons ago."

'Fayum sank to his knees and gazed up at his grandfather saying, "But the memory is still clear as fresh rainwater cupped in a green leaf and their story will live on...."

'The old elephant merely bowed low and rubbed his trunk along Fayum's body, encouraging him to stand. "Come," he said, "bring your good friend and we will feast your arrival."

'They feasted through the night on wild fruits and delicious resinated, juicy young barks. Fayum and Hugill did their circus act for the assembled gathering. And the loud stamping and trumpeting which greeted each trick, accompanied by Kush's shrieks and laughs, was pleasanter and sweeter to their ears than any circus audience of past experience. Towards dawn tranquillity settled upon the revellers. It was the grey time when the air chills suddenly and a hush falls over the land before the break of a new day. Into that silence filtered the haunting notes of Hugill's organ, through the trees and down to the slumbering villages. It was his farewell to Fayum.

"Ah my dear friend, if only you could stay," sighed Fayum.

'But Hugill only somersaulted once or twice, cocked his head to one side and gave his shoulders a sad little shrug. "Oh Fayum…we have covered many miles together in search of your beginnings…your family. But my search hasn't even begun. I don't know where I belong, or where my roots lie. It's certainly not in India; nor is it in the circus caravan of my birth. It is somewhere but where I don't know. So you see, I mustn't give up now."

"But should you ever have need, send word and I will come," persisted Fayum, wrapping his trunk around Hugill's middle as if he never wanted to let go of his friend.

'Hugill stroked the trunk and then kissed its soft fleshy tip gently. He twisted out of the elephant's hold and somersaulted to the edge of the forest. There he stood, his head cocked to one side and a hand raised in farewell. The two animals looked at each other for a long, long time, to store, forever, that last moment in each other's sight. And then Hugill was gone, his beloved organ on his back.

'Ahh…this is the life,' Grandfather sighed as he stretched out his legs and propped his head against his rucksack. He raised a small thimble of champagne to his lips and gulped the contents down noisily. 'Well to continue. Hugill hadn't gone very far when he was stopped by a rush of loud squawks and wails.

'It was Kush, of course, and he was hopping frantically from branch to branch above him shrieking: "You can't go without me you know! Not without me at all, at all, at all…you know. No!No!No! I'm not staying here! I've had enough of all these elephants and this endless jungle!"

'Hugill stopped and looked at the parrot.

"I think you should stay Kush. I'm an adventurer. I'm always looking for something and that means that I lead a very restless and aimless life."

"Suits me! Suits me!" squawked Kush.

'Hugill shrugged and the odd pair continued on through the jungle North-Eastwards.

"I'm thinking of climbing Everest," said Hugill one evening while sitting beneath a huge fig tree eating a wild fig.

"Nuts..nuts…nuts…that's what you are. It's too high…far too high." By now Kush was hopping in a frenzy from branch to branch above Hugill, who turned this way and that in an attempt to keep track of the bird.

"Kush! Kush! Keep still! You're making me dizzy. And stop repeating yourself. I had hoped that you would not interfere with my meanderings. If you don't want to join me then you are free to wait for me at the base. Besides, why do you think I've got long arms and legs?"

"Mmmmmum's the word…but you're still nuts," replied Kush, determined to have the last word before taking off into the highest branches of the tree.

'Hugill shrugged and went to sleep. Kush stayed high up in the trees only descending hours after sunrise to continue the journey, sometimes flying a little way behind Hugill, sometimes a little way ahead, but never just beside him. They continued in silence for the rest of the journey, quite a feat of endurance for Kush I can tell you. Towards nightfall, on the fifth day, they reached a forest in one of the valleys at the base of Everest. And that, my dear Livingstone, was where Hugill and I met!'

'What?' I asked in amazement, interrupting his long tale.

'Gha…gha…gha' he chuckled. 'That surprised you! It was during "The Columbus Mouse Everest Expedition of 1975." Your father and I were camping in a forest at the base of Everest waiting for a good day to begin our ascent. As I remember, the evening of our meeting was rather cool and the forest was thick with animal sounds which wafted unintelligibly towards us. We had just settled ourselves comfortably over a delicious meal of wheat bread, wild dates and groundnuts when we overheard the oddest conversation:

"Your long arms and legs are for climbing trees, not mountains. Besides, you can't carry that organ-thing up with you," said the one voice, high-pitched and rather birdlike.

"Oh Kush!" laughed the other, deeper voice. "Is that what you've been thinking about in such profound silence these last few days. You are very funny, you know."

"No I'm not…no I'm not…not…not…"

"Don't fall into repetitions. I apologise, but you ought to learn to laugh at yourself a bit more. It's the first step to becoming truly wise."

"What's the good of wisdom when you're lying at the bottom of a crevice with a broken organ on top of you? You tell me that, my wise friend."

'A silence followed.

"Well said Kush, but far too cautious for this life. It is unlikely to happen and think of how much we would have missed by not trying the mountain. Anyway, you worry about your wings and I'll worry about my arms and legs."

'Your father and I looked at each other in astonishment. Then, through the trees emerged a multicoloured parrot followed by a monkey carrying an organ. The parrot hopped around us in silence, eyeing our store of groundnuts. The monkey instantly darted forward, free hand outstretched saying: "Hugill Macauley, Hugill Macauley. How do you do…how do you do. This is my friend Kush."

'We introduced ourselves and invited them to join our small repast, and by the time the moon was high in the dark night sky, a rich and good friendship had grown between us all. We invited them to join our expedition and we all (including Kush!) climbed Everest successfully, despite Kush's continuous predictions of doom and disaster. Ahh… what a good time we had (but that's another story for another time). We spent many months travelling with them across Asia and then they returned with us to London, where they lived for a time. But Hugill Macauley was never one to stay in one place for long. Always an adventurer. Always searching for something. I've since heard of him walking the Great Wall of China from end to end, in search of a lost snake who had fled from his snake-charmer owner in Hong Kong because he had lost his ability to charm; and travelling in a canoe down the Amazon to visit some of Kush's cousins who were the only possessors of a trick to make parrots fly upside down; even crossing Mongolia on a camel rescued from an impoverished trader in Alexandria, and always accompanied by the obstinate and obstreperous Kush.'

Grandfather stopped to take a breath. 'Dear, dear Hugill…such a strange life. I do hope he finds it… whatever he's looking for.' He sighed and his tale came to an end, and so did our journey.

CHAPTER THREE

TERRA FIRMA

The plane landed. Africa at last!

'Hugill won't meet us in the ordinary manner, of that you can be quite sure,' said Grandfather, lifting his rucksack onto his back. 'That's because he's a firm believer in the hidden joys of the unexpected. So, there's no point in going out the way we came in.'

We waited until the crew were ready to depart the empty plane. Grandfather Darwin grabbed me by the paw and with a quick bound leapt onto the underside of an overnight case being pulled by one of the air hostesses. It wasn't long before we were both on the pavement outside the airport. There we sat in a shady spot to await the unexpected. And, as with all adventures, it was not long in coming. In the corner of my eye I detected a movement. I looked round and there, a little distance away, I saw a placard attached to a stick. It was unmistakeably moving rapidly up and down. I gazed at the placard for some time and finally made out the following words in bold, black print:

FOLLOW ME! ME! ME!

There was something oddly familiar about those words, so I decided to investigate. I approached the placard but as soon as I came within a few feet, it moved steadily backwards. I tried to creep round it but it moved round to face me. I tried to dodge the other way but it quickly turned to face me again. I decided to speak to it, bearing in mind my suspicions: 'Hello! Hello! Is that Mr Kush behind the placard?'

Silence. Then the placard fluttered off the ground and sank down again. 'What if it is? What if it is?' came a squawked reply.

'Well, it is important if you are, because you've probably come to meet us…Grandfather Darwin and Livingstone, the Mice from Leicester Square Underground.'

Silence again. Then a bright yellow and red face peered out from behind the placard. A luminous green wing followed.

I shook the wing delicately having never really shaken a bird by the wing before and said: 'How do you do…I'm Livingstone.'

'Good! Good! Now where's your intrepid Grandfather?' came the reply and that was that: my first meeting with Kush.

I lead him to Grandfather where the formalities of wing and paw-shaking were begun again, amidst much animated squawking and many elevations from the ground.

'Oh dear, dear Kush! How good to see you! Where's Hugill?' asked Grandfather peering behind the placard.

'Oh, he's not here I'm afraid. Sends his apologies. Said to give you this message.' And deep from within his feathers, Kush drew out a piece of paper and handed it to Grandfather, who spread it out on the ground. On it was a map of the Rift Valley, below which was written a curious message which Grandfather read aloud:

Beginnings are never where or what they seem
and they might never end.
But we are searching for a beginning to this story
and North is where we'll start.
So, follow a fine-feathered friend to a verdant lake's papyrus-sedge shore.

'Vintage Hugill,' laughed Grandfather. 'Seems to be nonsensical, but full of sense I'm sure.'

'He means Lake Naivasha, of course. It stands to reason…that's where he was going when he sent me back to meet you,' said Kush in rather a huff. 'Typical!' he then said, taking off and landing above us on the top of a parked taxi.

'Dear Kush, literal to the last. I'm sure he means much more than that, we'll see. But do come down and let's begin our adventure,' said Grandfather. The slightly plaintive edge to his plea proved irresistible and Kush descended regally to take up position as our *fine-feathered* leader.

We checked over our rucksacks and set off in high excitement. We put the city behind us and spent the rest of the day marching across an undulating terrain of mixed vegetation, sometimes brown and dull green scrub, at other times forested slopes. The going was hard and rough. We tried not to think too much of our water-bottles and the delicious klinking noise the water made as we walked along. 'Get used to doing without,' Grandfather had told me before we started. He was quite right, we had to preserve our small supply, but how hard it was at times to obey. And dear Kush was always there, encouraging us along or rushing ahead to find us easier routes and hidden pathways through the undergrowth.

The night, our first in Africa, came as a welcome relief from the long day's exertions. Like a cool dark blue-black cloak, it settled around us very suddenly. And when the stars appeared, Grandfather excitedly handed me the binoculars, pointing out Orion's Belt (with Betelguese and Rigel) and Canopus and Syrius and many, many more scattered across that great expanse of sky; glistening pinpricks of light which filled my binocular vision. From far off we heard a solitary leopard growl into the night; a hyena giggled close-by; a bat fluttered around us, bright eyes staring and then the air became dense with sound of crickets. I trembled from whisker to tail and huddled closer to Grandfather, wrapping his long tail around my waist for added protection.

Just before dropping to sleep he sighed and then spoke in awe: 'This journey is taking us into the great Rift Valley, Livingstone. I have always wanted to see it.'

We awoke at first light. The air was still cool and fresh, like softly running water. The light—of a luminous brightness—seemed to dance and ripple along the very tips of the dry grasses. After a light snack we continued our march. Our progress was slow and we rested frequently, taking small sips from our water-bottles. A heady mixture of unknown odours rose up around us, distilled no doubt by the heat. Then, quite suddenly, the generally noisy undergrowth went strangely silent. Birds overhead moved away quickly. Even the warm breeze whistling through the shrub seemed to die, leaving the leaves and grasses upright, as if expectantly waiting. We came to a halt, though we were not sure why.

Into that deadened silence came a sharp crackle of twigs, followed by a hoarse, rasping cough. 'Eek!' screeched Kush, disappearing into a nearby bush. Grandfather moved close to me and put a protective arm round my shoulders, squeezing me to absolute stillness. We froze. Another loud cough punctured that suffocating hush, then a hot panting breath. Its rank stench nearly overpowered us. The long dry grasses suddenly parted and to my horror I found myself looking at a livid pink tongue—long and wet—and then into the frightening yellow eye of a young male leopard! My knees gave way and I sank to the ground.

The leopard came nearer, pushing his way rudely through the grasses. He dropped his head down to us and snorted. Grandfather pulled me behind him and he faced the huge leopard-leer and those black-ringed eyes which followed every minute movement we made. The leopard grumbled and then spoke: 'They that leaves me alone will be left alone by me. Pass a message on to some mouse called Darwin indeed! Who be this Hugill anyway, telling me who I'm to meet and that conversation would be good for me? I don't likes talking, I don't likes people and I don't likes silly animals getting in my way.' Another deep cough followed this coarse, cross speech and he brushed past, one huge paw narrowly missing us! His claws were so close to my tail, that I could see their menacing inward curl as they sank into the earth.

Like a bright light going on, the world around us became noisy and busy once again. From the nearby bush came a loud chattering. It was Kush of course. In a flurry of feathers and leaves he emerged, talking and repeating himself. 'Well, what do you think? What do you think? Hugill's nuts…nuts…Leopards! Leopards are the most secretive and solitary of all the animals. They don't even like each other very much.'

'But,' said Grandfather, interrupting the flow, 'there seems to be another message for us somewhere. I wonder what it is?' We all went silent on that note and continued our journey until nightfall and set up camp. It was definitely a night for Grandfather's restorative wholemeal biscuits and the three of us feasted royally. Gradually the frightening image of those searing yellow eyes so close to our own became blurred and faded to a distant reminder.

I lay curled close to Grandfather, looking up at the cornucopia display of stars. There were many more animal sounds to be heard now that we had ventured further into the Southern end of the Rift Valley: the howl of a jackal; the kloo-ee ku-lee of an eagle (could it be Warrior or was he somewhere far off?); the ever-present crickets; the bark of a baboon scout and a host of unrecognisable growls and shrieks and whoopees, all becoming slightly muffled as the night pressed in on us. How far this was from our home on the Underground, I thought as I drowsed comfortably under the broad African sky.

CHAPTER FOUR
LOSING SIGHT OF THINGS

The following morning did not begin well. Kush overslept and forgot to wake us up with his usual squawks and repetitions. Then he disappeared towards a clump of tall acacias some distance away, mumbling something about delicious, irresistible berries he had overheard two hornbills discussing the evening before. That was not all: Grandfather had mislaid his binoculars. They must have fallen in the long grass while we set up camp in the dark. We decided to separate in our search, keeping a gnarled and bare thorn-bush in view as our meeting point.

We parted company. Very soon I became quite lost in the long grass. And when I looked for our tree, I discovered that where I had seen one before, I now saw three! All twisted and misshapen, like three tired old travellers resting awhile. I walked in the direction of the nearest one, hoping it was the right one. I was almost there when I heard it…a hoarse dry cough. I fell backwards in the grass. Oh no! It was the leopard! What was I to do? I lay very still for a long time, waiting for the rustle of disturbed grasses to subside. When all seemed calm I peered through the stalks. I could just make out the brown, black and orange markings on what looked like the leopard's tail. I rolled onto my stomach and crawled backwards. Just when I thought I had succeeded in getting away I came up hard against one of his paws. I leapt to one side and turned to face him, quaking with terror. He seemed to be asleep, but then he opened one yellow eye and stared at me.

I was so frightened I couldn't move away from that fearsome leer and those huge claws. I couldn't even speak. We both remained silent for what seemed a long time. Then I had an idea. I decided to take his mind off me and to focus it on something else. So, moving with what I hoped was imperceptible slowness, and expecting to be swallowed whole any second, I lifted my magnifying glass and gazed at him through it.

He frowned and squinted at the glass. 'What be that?' he asked, his gruff voice lifting a little in surprise.

'It's a magnifying glass.'

'With what to do?'

'To make things bigger with.'

The leopard laughed a deep, dry laugh. 'What do you want with making me bigger for?' and then he held out a leisurely paw. I handed him the glass and he put it up to one eye, gazing at me through it. Then he exclaimed:

'Why! You be twice your size...and be easier to look at...I can stop my squinting and frowning.' The leopard continued to look at me through the magnifying glass. 'What you be looking for then with this thing?'

'Well, um...a pair of binoculars.'

'A what?'

Oh dear, how was I to explain? 'Uhmmm...it's another kind of glass. If you look through the one end it helps you to bring things closer and then you can see what things that are far away are really like. If you look through the other end, it makes things look smaller, further away.'

The leopard laughed again. 'What an odd lot you be. Why not live a simple life like me and content yourselves with your own eyes!'

'Oh no!' I replied. 'It makes life much more exciting... it changes the world, helps you to see things in a new and different way. Besides, look how it has helped you to talk to me more easily, now that I'm twice my size and you can see me better.'

'Um...' went the leopard, now looking at me rather suspiciously through the magnifying glass. 'But I don't reckon that I want to see things in a new way. I don't like change, I like things just as they are.'

'How dull and uneventful.'

But the leopard wasn't listening. He was looking through the glass at a beetle climbing up the length of a frond of dry grass. Then he gazed at a tiny earthworm slithering past his paws and then at an ant-hole in a thorn tree. Suddenly he found his own paws a great source of fascination. First he looked at one spot and then at another, and another. 'My spots!' He exclaimed at length. 'My spots! They be changing!'

'No they haven't. It's just that you're seeing more into them…all the different colours that make them up. You see, that's what I mean: change is so interesting.'

'Mmmm...' said the leopard, nodding his head slowly. 'Now what about that other glass of yours? I want to see it.'

'We have to find it first,' I replied.

The leopard thought for a minute and then, with slight reluctance, he handed me the glass and lifted me gently onto his neck.

We walked slowly through the tall grass. My body rocked to his measured and rhythmical padding. The grass-tips tickled my nose; the birds flew around us, inquisitive to see what was going on. The leopard made for a high rocky outcrop. His long powerful body moved gracefully from rock to rock until he reached the top. From there we were able to survey the whole terrain. The leopard narrowed his eyes and looked long and hard in every direction. With a slight inclination of his head he pointed towards Grandfather, scuttling this way and that through the grass, as I had been; then he directed his gaze at Kush guzzling berries in a tree; and lastly at something glinting in the grass, not far from our campsite. It was the binoculars!

So, down we went again. The leopard padded over to Grandfather who scurried backwards in shock and fear until, with a look of complete surprise, he saw me on the leopard's neck. He worked his way up the leopard's leg towards me and was about to ply me with questions when he saw me put my paw to my mouth. We padded over to where we had seen the binoculars lying in the grass. Sure enough, there they were. The leopard sank gently to the ground, off-loaded us and immediately picked them up.

Grandfather looked at me questioningly.

'Shsh...' I whispered.

Meanwhile the leopard gazed at the world through Grandfather's binoculars, first through one end and then through the other. Then he swung it round his neck and galloped back towards the rocky outcrop, disappearing from sight.

'But...but...Livingstone...he's pinched my binoculars.'

'No...I don't think so...I think...yes...yes...look...I'm right...' and we looked up at the rock. There he was at the top, a magnificent dark silhouette against the sky, sitting on his haunches and gazing through the binoculars at the vast plain below him, edged by the high valley walls. He gazed at the sky, at the sun, at the huge shifting clouds...as if to draw them all nearer, to hold them in his powerful grip.

He disappeared from view again and was soon by our side. He handed Grandfather the binoculars and looked at me and laughed dryly. 'Can you send me one of those eye-glass things like yours, one that's for my size?'

'Of course,' I replied. 'When I get back to London I'll see that Kush brings one to you.'

'Eek!' came a shriek from above us. It was Kush and he seemed to have appeared from nowhere, a tell-tail berry disappearing down his throat. He took one look at the leopard and prepared to dive into a bush, when I shouted to him to stop.

'Don't worry, this is a new friend of mine,' and I looked inquiringly at the leopard, who merely dropped his lids over yellow eyes. Kush was clearly still uneasy with this close encounter with a leopard. He rustled his feathers and flew into the lowest branch of the nearby thorn-tree…a polite enough distance away.

Grandfather turned to the leopard. 'You don't have any sort of message for us do you?'

The leopard shook his head. 'Didn't take it in none too much…mmm…but this Hugill fellow did say something about 'change' (and the leopard looked at me meaningfully), or was it 'a change…a change in plan?' Not sure. But that were all.'

'Oh dear,' said Grandfather. 'We'd better be on our way.'

The leopard nodded and moved off casually into the grass. Before disappearing completely, he stopped and swung his head round to face me: 'Now don't you forget…about that eye-glass,' and he winked imperceptibly and was gone.

'Phew!' Kush sighed, descending from the thorn-tree. 'I think we should have some of those special biscuits of yours Darwin. I can never get used to leopards, never, never, never, and now my nerves are all shaken up; quite, quite shaken up…and I will need an afternoon rest...'

While he prepared the meal, Grandfather looked into the far distance and mumbled to me: 'Mmm…Hugill's messages are becoming rather mysterious Livingstone… change…a change in plan…now I wonder what he meant by that?'

I certainly had an idea or two, about the leopard that is.

CHAPTER FIVE

OBSERVATIONS

Something was not quite right. I even sensed it while deeply asleep. I had the distinct feeling that I was being watched. I awoke with a start and shivered slightly in the cool afternoon breeze.

I was quite right. Directly in front of me, about three feet away, was an eye; a large black eye framed by delicate cinnamon coloured eyelashes. The eye was staring straight at me. It belonged to a ball-shaped head which ended in a rather sharp beak. The head was perched on top of a long, thin (pink-thin) neck. When it moved, as it suddenly did, it looked oddly like a periscope, balanced precariously on a glistening-grassy wave. The head turned to face the other way and treated me to another long stare from the other black eye.

Surely it could not be a snake, snakes didn't end in beaks? What was it? By now the neck was rising and falling somewhat agitatedly, but throughout its prancing either one of those two black eyes never ceased its alert surveillance.

I jerked Grandfather's tail and his eyes flew open in alarm. I motioned to him to remain still. 'We're being watched,' I whispered.

He frowned and looked ahead through his binoculars. The long neck was quite still again, the eye now staring at Grandfather, who in turn gazed back at it. Then Grandfather burst out laughing. 'Why, it's an ostrich!' he guffawed.

'Where? Where?' shrieked Kush, waking suddenly and nearly falling out of the thorn bush.

'There!' pointed Grandfather.

But as he did so there was an unexpected rush and rustle of grasses and a zebra suddenly appeared from nowhere, placing herself protectively in front of the ostrich. Then she sniffed the air around us and moved a few paces nearer, sniffing the grass all the time. In another rush, she turned back to the ostrich. 'Well done my dear Sappho, you've found them! Those eyes of yours are really quite remarkable.'

'Thank you Aurelia,' said the ostrich shyly, moving forward so that we could see the rest of her: a large bulbous brown-feathered body perched on the spindliest of legs and webbed feet. It was definitely a bird, but quite the oddest bird I had ever seen.

They both turned to smile at us and the zebra said sweetly: 'We share our senses.'

'What's that?' squawked Kush.

'Well,' she said, 'life in Africa can be somewhat hectic. You see lions seem to have taken a liking to my stripes and leopards rather enjoy ostriches. One day we discovered that Sappho could see rather better than I could, whereas I could hear and smell rather better than she could. So we joined forces, as it were. And it's worked rather well, we've been eating herbs and grasses quite peacefully together on this plain for many years.'

'Do you mean to tell me,' said Grandfather, 'that two such entirely different species -- a bird and a mammal -- have been living in peaceful co-existence for some length of time?'

'Yes,' replied the zebra simply.

'Oh what a lovely word Aurelia,' said the ostrich. 'Co-existence, peaceful co-existence, how very fine it sounds,' and she pirouetted on her long spindly legs saying the word 'co-existence' to herself over and over again, giving rise to a flurry of dust and a spray of dry grasses at the same time.

The zebra turned to Grandfather. 'Is it so very unusual amongst animals?'

'Well, mutual agreement over a long period of time is truly remarkable, even amongst members of the same species. I know of one species of animal whose members can't seem to get along at all,' replied Grandfather taking a notebook and pencil out of his rucksack and writing it all down.

'Oh dear, what a pity,' replied the zebra sadly.

Meanwhile the ostrich stopped her wild little dance and shyly whispered something in the zebra's ear.

'Oh yes, the message,' said the zebra and she turned to us again. 'We heard that the silly old leopard wouldn't deliver it. So we offered.'

'What is it? What is it?' asked Kush loudly.

'Here it is...but I can't say that I fully grasp the meaning of it.' She bent low and we moved closer to her soft black mouth to listen. This is what she said:

A tangential course can be of great use: the tangent to our tale so far has been found on a sensory plane, to find the rest search a lava slope for a Perceiver of the Furthest Distance.

Baffled, we all looked at one another.

'Nuts...Hugill's lost his marbles,' sighed Kush taking off into the thorn tree.

'I don't think so. He looked quite normal to us, didn't he Sappho?' said the zebra.

'Yes Aurelia, as normal as a monkey with an organ on his back could look on an African plain I suppose,' replied the ostrich, the merest hint of doubt in her voice. 'But the sensory plane must refer to us I think...how sweet of him...' and she smiled shyly again.

'And the leopard,' I interjected.

'Shhh...' Kush shouted down at me, ruffling his feathers.

'Mmmm...do you know Livingstone, it's all becoming rather like a treasure hunt,' mused Grandfather pulling at his whiskers. 'Hugill at his most wizardly seems to be unfolding a story via a treasure hunt. Take this message: it's not only helping us to find him, but it's also pointing out hidden treasures along the way---delightful animal treasures; treasures requiring careful observation. Gha... gha... gha' he laughed suddenly, slapping his thigh. 'Now we have to find a steamy slope...I wonder where that could be?' and he rubbed his paws together in excitement and then settled on the grass to write the message down in his notebook.

'Longonot!' shrieked Kush after a while.

'What?' we all asked, looking up to where he was perched in the thorn bush.

'Lava....slopes...volcanoes...nearest volcano in line with Naivasha...Longonot...stands to reason ...' he said disdainfully.

'Oh, well done Kush!' shouted Grandfather. 'Please come down and let me shake your wing.'

Kush descended proudly and we all crowded round him to compliment him on his clever piece of deduction. Grandfather pulled out his map and studied it for a while. 'Yes, here it is...the Volcano of Longonot. We have to bear North-East. And look, it's on Hugill's map too. Now where's the compass?' He searched in his rucksack again and drew out the shiny brass compass, turning it this way and that until he had the correct bearing.

'Goodbye and good luck my dears,' said the zebra, giving us a little nod before turning away.

The ostrich dropped her head down and nuzzled each of us in turn with her hard strange beak. Then she rolled her sinuous neck up and pranced off, still whispering 'peaceful co-existence…oh how very fine it sounds.'

We waved goodbye to the two animals as they went off together across the plain and then turned away ourselves, bearing North-East and in the direction of the Volcano of Longonot.

'Perceiver of the Furthest Distance…mmmm…,' mumbled Grandfather to himself as we walked on through the tall grasses.

We decided to walk on through the night to cover as much distance as we could over the plain. The sky gradually changed: the bright blue faded to a soft pink, the pink to a rich coppery-red. The land seemed to stretch itself out beneath the sky, to throw up its wares: blackened acacia branches reached out; broken-bent thorn trees bowed as if in homage; animals were stilled, eyes turned heavenwards.

It was a strange night of no wind, of a sultriness which hung heavily about us. The animals kept their distance and we spoke to no-one. We could feel that they were there, an animal sense of presences, though there was no movement and certainly no hunting or searching was done that night. They were all preoccupied, waiting. For what? We didn't know, but the answer lay in the sky and the air. It told them all they needed to know, but we of the foreign Northern Climes couldn't read it, except to be aware.

Morning came at last. But it brought no relief from the hot air. And still there was no wind. The sky was punctured with large clumps of bulbous grey clouds which grouped and regrouped continuously, like heavy lumps of clay, casting strangely shaped shadows across the plain. The bits of blue between had a purple haze…quite unlike the bright morning sky we had become used to.

Then the whistling began, a soft haunting melody from far off at first, which grew louder and louder, to a piercing, howling crescendo.

'The thorn trees,' whispered Kush, now subdued and tending to hover close to us. 'It's the wind whistling through them.' But it was not a welcome wind. The heat had reached such an intensity that it felt as if the earth would crack beneath us. I wanted to run and hide, to shut off that piercing noise…but where? All the land was exposed, but to what?

The animals drifted into separate clusters. Nearby some gazelles hovered together, sharp horns pointed now at the sky now towards each other; herds of zebra and buffalo huddled close and stayed very still; in the far distance three massive elephants tramped slowly across the darkening plain as if wading through thick dull air. The whistling wind continued to ripple and run low across the grass and bush until, as suddenly as it had come, so it left, as if swallowed by the black sky itself. All went silent again.

Then a loud boom roared across the sky and threw itself on the earth. A deafening crack followed and the rain fell! In great slanting gushes it fell. A streak of lightening suddenly tore the black clouds apart, striking an old acacia tree and irradiating it for a moment before disappearing. A withered branch of the tree began a slow arc towards the ground, leaving a raw, gaping wound.

Kush cleverly directed us towards the edge of a forest and we buried ourselves deep in the undergrowth. It rained all that day and the next and the next...three days it rained in all; a vast ocean of water given up at last to the great hot absorbing land.

We remained hidden while the storm raged and fell about us, quite dry but for the odd trickle which managed to find us out. And we were not alone: a large grey rock-rabbit had joined us. He crawled in, apologised for taking up so much room, curled himself into a ball and fell asleep.

On the evening of the third day the storm suddenly ceased. It just stopped, as if the contents of the heavens had been emptied out. The wet earth sighed and fell back into itself, becalmed now and laden with water. The grey clouds began to move off slowly like some tired army at the end of a hard battle.

The rock-rabbit woke up and shook himself all over. He peered out of the thicket and then turned to us. 'Well, that's that then,' he said with a slight shrug. 'The lakes will be full now, thank goodness, and the rock pools.' Then he looked more closely at us. 'Ah you must be the Mice from Leicester Square and Kush the parrot. Ah ha.' And he nodded his head.

'Do you know about us?' asked Grandfather in surprise.

'Oh a rumour here and there,' he replied and disappeared into the thicket.

CHAPTER SIX

A LIGHT IN THE DARK

We crawled out of the undergrowth and walked to the edge of the forest. It was on high ground and we were able to survey the whole area. The air was cool. The land had lost its dry, shimmering expectancy and was now softer to the eye. A pale disc-shaped moon appeared and the clouds, which were very high, stretched in thin threads across a lilac sky.

The animals, now unrecognisable in the evening light, walked desultorily across the plain, unhurried and quite unperturbed. Some returned to the patch of grass they had been nibbling before it all began; others drifted towards the pools which now dotted the grasslands. A calm had descended: once again the great earth would be able to provide for its dwellers.

We turned back into the forest. How it glistened and trembled with the millions of water-drops, which hung in intricate web-like patterns on bushes and thickets, or dropped delicately from the leaves of huge, unending trees. And everywhere the sound of running water competed loudly with the birdsong so that it seemed that the aftermath of the earth-shaking storm had produced a great lightening of the spirit. And as we listened, we heard, from far away, the haunting notes of an organ. Was it another message, of encouragement perhaps? Or was it just an expression of the way we all felt after the storm? How could we know? But it did bring us closer to the elusive Hugill Macauley.

Kush turned to us, his little black eyes sparking. 'He's out there somewhere…somewhere South of here I think. Yes, yes, yes, I do think so.' And he nodded and repeated himself in his excitement.

'But that's odd,' said Grandfather. 'He sent us North to find a story's beginning and then on a *tangent* to the North-East to find a *Perceiver of the Furthest Distance* and yet he is somewhere South of here. How very odd it all is. But that's Hugill Macauley! Anyway, whatever else we have to do, first we have to find this *tangent*. I wonder who that could be?'

We walked deeper into the forest. The air was rich with unknown fragrances. The trees were wrapped in a tangle of creeper and fungus which hung and drooped low to the ground, filling the forest with ancient and hidden mystery. The ground was covered in a thick carpet of moss, spongy underfoot. The night closed in, intensely black now that we were cut off from the moon and stars;

though sometimes we managed to catch a glimpse of them here and there, shining through the leaves or reflected in the odd pool of water.

We struggled through the dense undergrowth and creeper, drawn deeper into the darkness.

'I think we're lost,' wailed Kush, dropping down heavily beside us.

Grandfather took out his torch and peered at the compass. 'Yes…yes…we're moving too far to the East, we'll have to change direction.' So we turned and headed Northwards.

'Ha!…ha!…ha! Lost are you? Ha!…ha!…ha!' squeaked a shrill voice suddenly from the surrounding blackness. We stopped dead in our tracks and looked around. 'Ha!…ha!…ha!' came the voice again. But still we could not see anything. 'I only startle you know… for fun…I wouldn't eat you. Couldn't eat you as a matter of fact. Those bags on your back would stop me for one thing. Ha!…ha!…ha!' The thing went silent for a while and then it said: 'Would you like some wild figs, I know just the place and it's not far from here?'

Kush immediately perked up and the thing laughed again. Then we saw a black form hanging from a branch above, swinging backwards and forwards.

'Ha!…ha!…ha! You've found me. Well done,' and with that a bat circled around us and then fluttered down to a lower branch and hung himself upside down, his wings settling around him like a dusky-black cloak.

He was quite a big creature, certainly bigger than Kush. Bigger than any bat I had ever seen. He had a small face and big dark eyes which darted this way and that and then at us; first at Kush and then at Grandfather and me, beginning with our tails and working all the way along to our whisker-tips. 'Ha!...ha!...ha!' he laughed again, rocking backwards and forwards. 'My name's Fu and how do you do, Darwin and Livingstone Mices and parroty Kush,' and he gave an extra large rock, quite disappearing into the foliage for a while. He returned with another 'ha!...ha!...ha!' and then said: 'Now how about a wild fig? You must be sick of the food you keep pulling out of those bags on your back.'

'Oh we are! We are!' wailed Kush.

'We would love some,' replied Grandfather.

'Well, come on then,' said Fu and he led us deeper into the forest, to a large and heavily laden fig-tree. He fluttered up to a comfortable looking branch and beckoned to us to follow with encouraging squeaks and ha!...ha!...has!

'Delicious...mmm...delicious,' mumbled Kush hopping from fig to fig, and eating at a great rate. He was quite right, they were slightly over-ripe and deliciously syrupy; a wonderful change from our rations of biscuits and dried sausage.

Meanwhile, Fu flew to a branch above us and hung down, his wide eyes watching us all the time. It was most disconcerting having someone look at one from upside down, especially while one's mouth was full.

'How did you know where to look for us?' asked Grandfather.

'Oh this funny monkey friend of yours asked me to look out for you. As a matter of fact I had a jolly good look at you all on your first night in Africa,' replied Fu.

'Was that you?' I interrupted, remembering the bat that had fluttered around us that night.

Fu nodded and continued: 'Your friend thought I'd come in handy, particularly if you tried walking through this forest at night. A silly thing to do of course, but if you must you must and I can at least help you.'

'How?' I asked.

'Oh with my eyes: I can see perfectly in the dark and my hearing's not too bad either,' replied Fu.

'Did Hugill…our friend that is, say anything else, anything at all?' asked Grandfather.

'No,' said Fu, 'just to see you safely through the forest and to deposit you at the base of the volcano.'

'Ahh, so we *are* going to the Volcano of Longonot. You are not by any chance the *Perceiver of the Furthest Distance*?'

'I don't know what you're talking about,' said Fu shaking his upside-down head at us. 'But how odd, who is it?'

'We don't know. It was part of Hugill's last message to us.'

'I can't say I've ever met a *Perceiver of the Furthest Distance*, quite an odd name I must say.'

I had eaten my fill of figs and decided to try hanging upside down too. I wound my tail-end round the branch three times, pulling tight to secure it and then I let go. At first I swung wildly, the ground beneath moving dizzily near and then breathtakingly far. Then gradually I began to slow down and the world sort of righted itself, or rather wronged itself rightfully the wrong way (if you see what I mean?). It was quite a pleasant sensation at first but then I began to feel rather ill. Perhaps it was those figs. All of a sudden I could no longer keep my tail around the branch. I tried to stop it from unwinding, but it had a life of its own and down I plunged. Instead of a hard landing, I found myself trapped in a soft black web. It was Fu and he had caught me in one of his wings.

'Ha!...ha!...ha!' he laughed. 'You have to be geared or wired for that sort of thing. But a nice try anyway.' And he carried me back to Grandfather and Kush who were both laughing so hard that they too came perilously close to falling from the branch.

'Time to move on if you want to be at the base of the volcano by morning,' said Fu.

So we left the welcome confines of the fig tree and followed him through the forest, bearing North-East. How wise and clever Hugill was to have sent so able a navigator I thought, as Fu darted backwards and forwards, encouraging us along with his shrill whistles and squeaks. Once or twice he stopped to listen to the forest, his head moving up and down, this way and that as he checked the trees and the undergrowth for hidden dangers or unexpected surprises.

With the coming of the pale grey-pink dawn we had our first sighting of the volcano. We had reached a clearing and there it lay before us, its high-domed form towering massively above; its thickly forested slope a dark velvety green in the ghostly early morning light. And there was a misty haze at the top, coming no doubt from within the bowels of the volcano itself. I felt a cold shiver run down my spine to my tail-end at the thought of what adventures lay ahead.

Fu fluttered to a branch above us and hung down. 'Well, my friends, my part in your journey ends here,' he said regretfully, noticing our worried frowns as we contemplated the volcano.

'I wish you were coming with us,' I said to his encouraging upside-down face. Fu just shook his head and rocked backwards and forwards.

'I don't like this Longonot place at all…at all…at all…' wailed Kush, his whole body beginning to shake.

'Come along old fellow, we can't stop now,' said Grandfather patting his wing-tip.

We thanked Fu for guiding us through the forest and for showing us the hoard of wild figs. He rocked faster and turned his face away. So we waved goodbye and with a heavy sigh faced the volcano.

We began to walk across the clearing towards the base. Grandfather was soon way ahead. Kush and I followed reluctantly, he flying just above me. We stopped frequently to gaze in awe at the densely covered slope, at the haze floating mysteriously around the crater. After a while Grandfather noticed that we had fallen behind and that we both looked rather dispirited. When we reached him he rubbed his paws together and said: 'Some biscuits, I think!' Our spirits revived at the very idea of it and by the time breakfast was over we felt a great deal better about the task of finding the *Perceiver* on that forbidding slope.

We were just about to set off again when we saw the strangest of sights: at one end of the clearing were two handsome, long-necked impala, their powerful curled horns locked in fierce combat and their eyes squinting as they stared angrily at each other. They pawed the ground a few times and then, with stiff movements, forced each other backwards and forwards. Dotted around them were the rest of the family: elegant females with exquisitely pointed ears and long smooth bodies and their brown-eyed young rubbing up close to them. They quietly nibbled the grass or pulled at leaves, not paying the slightest bit of attention to the battle in their midst. Grandfather immediately walked over to the group.

'Is there anything we can do to stop them from fighting?' he asked. The largest female detached herself and came over to him.

'Oh, it's no use stopping them,' she said, glancing over her shoulder at the two combatants. 'They do it this time every year.'

'But...but why?' I asked.

'I don't know...something just seems to overcome them once a year and they fight. It's rather silly because they're brothers and during the rest of the year they get on quite well. When this odd need to fight wells up in them they forget everything.'

'Haven't you ever tried to separate them?' asked Grandfather.

'Oh no, once those horns lock then it's impossible...I think that's why the fight goes on for so long. It can last for days. All quite, quite senseless...' and she turned lazily back to nibble at a bush.

Grandfather wrote a few notes in his notebook mumbling: 'Very odd...very odd behaviour indeed...'

The three of us shrugged and walked on, totally unnoticed by the two fighters.

CHAPTER SEVEN
LONGONOT

It was mid-morning when we reached the base of Longonot. By now the crater was lost in the sky and we had before us thick bush and a long climb in search of the *Perceiver.*

We began to work our way up. The ground felt wet possibly because of the heavy rains we had just had. It had a strange odour too, of a dark and mouldy fish-pond. And it was hard going. In desperation Kush flew high above the tangled mass of foliage to try and find a path for us from the air. He was soon lost to view---it was no good, we'd have to find a route through on our own. So we struggled on, becoming hot and bothered and despairing of ever finding what it was Hugill wanted us to find.

'Kush!' shouted Grandfather suddenly. 'Why don't you fly around the base and see if you can see the *Perceiver*?'

Kush looked horrified at the idea. 'But…I don't know what I'm looking for!'

'Don't worry...if this *Perceiver* can perceive then it will find you.'

'But...but...but I don't want to be found by it at all, at all!'

'No buts...off you go,' said Grandfather sternly.

Kush took off in a flurry of feathers and angry shrieks. We sat on a small log and waited. The trees stood out at odd angles on the slope, some leaning so far over that they looked as if they would fall on top of us.

'It's no use. No use at all!' came a loud wail and Kush sank down to us on the log. 'I can't find this *Perceiver* thing and clearly it hasn't found me. Let's go to the lake. I've had enough...I don't think I'm going to like this volcano. Besides, I think Hugill's nuts.' And with that he flew onto a branch of a nearby thorn tree and turned his face away from us.

Grandfather and I looked at each other and sighed. It was no use going on while Kush was in a sulk; we'd have to wait until he came out of it. We sat down again and drank some water from our water bottles. As it turned out we didn't have to wait too long for him to change his mind, because he suddenly hissed down to us: 'Quick, look left! Look left!'

We obeyed and looked around to our left. At first we couldn't see very much at all through the undergrowth, but then we discerned something that did look different. Was it an unusual bark of a tree, or rather, two long thin trees? They were certainly brown, but there were also bits of white too, the whole forming an intricate patchwork pattern. And they seemed to be swaying gently towards us.

'Ahem,' came a soft voice from somewhere at the top of the trees.

We looked up… and then up and up and up and up. Grandfather whipped up his binoculars and gazed up at the animal that gazed so resignedly down at us. Then he passed them on to me, whispering, 'It's a giraffe!' I could see that the brown markings in-between the white lines were much darker and bigger on her body and long graceful neck. And she had two tufted horns and a large hump where her forehead should have been. Her ears jutted straight out just behind her exquisitely shaped dark eyes and her long nose tapered to a soft, gently rounded mouth.

'The *Perceiver of the Furthest Distance*…of course! I should have realized,' said Grandfather, hitting his forehead. The giraffe inclined her head. 'Is there any way in which we could get a bit nearer to you, to the top of you I mean?' asked Grandfather. 'You see it's just that my neck is beginning to ache looking so far up.'

'Of course…I do apologise,' the giraffe replied languidly, her voice deep and resonant. She sedately stretched her forelegs wide open and gradually lowered her head down to us. 'Do climb onto my horns,' she said. And we did, Grandfather and Kush placing themselves on her horns and I on the hump in front. Slowly and with infinite care she began to pull her head up. The wind rushed past in a flurry and the trees and foliage danced and swirled around us in a blur. At last she was up and the world settled back into its old calm pattern again. And what a wonderful view we now had! We could see the dense vegetation lying far below us; we could see over the tops of high bushes and some of the trees; across the plain to the forest, to the glade where the impala still ambled.

'Oh Perceiver!' breathed Grandfather, looking at the world anew through his binoculars. 'How clever Hugill was to have introduced us.'

'Well, at least we don't have to smell that wet earth,' said Kush settling back comfortably on her horn.

'Could you see us struggling to find you?' I asked, leaning a little over to one side so that I could look into her eye.

'Yes. That's the problem in my life,' the Perceiver sighed, rather sadly I thought.

'What is?' I asked.

'Well, I never get a surprise…I always know what's going to happen next. Giraffes are the tallest of all the animals. That means that I could see you in the clearing and then I watched you struggling in the bush; I know when there's going to be a storm before any of the other animals have even noticed a change in the weather; I know every horizon; I know what's coming from the East, the West, the North and the South; I know when danger is near; I know and perceive almost before I know and perceive what it is that I know and perceive. And what I want most in life is a really good surprise,' and she sighed again, inclining her head and fluttering her soft black eyelashes.

'Surprise! Surprise! Who wants a surprise? I've had enough surprises on this adventure already,' said Kush, turning round and round on his perch.

'No,' said Grandfather. 'I can sympathise with the Perceiver. Being very small ourselves we can never be sure what's going to happen next and that makes for a great deal of excitement.'

The giraffe nodded and with a stately air began to pace up the slope. 'Your monkey friend asked me to carry you to the crater of Longonot,' she said.

'Thank goodness,' sighed Kush.

'Was there no other message?' asked Grandfather.

'Yes. He asked me to carry you up to the top of Longonot, to see you safely down again and then to go with you to the shores of Lake Naivasha. He also said I would know when I was no longer needed. That was all. Well no, not quite all...he said a few other things which I couldn't really understand at the time...I forget them now,' and she continued up the slope.

'Have you ever been to the top of Longonot?' I asked the Perceiver.

'No...it's something I have always been rather afraid of doing. Besides, I see from such a height anyway, I've never really wanted to go any higher to see more.'

By midday we had reached the rim of the crater and turned to face the way we had come. The great land opened up before us: the forest below and beyond that the rolling plain; in the distance the fringe of blue Rift Valley mountains; to the North we could just make out the green waters of a lake. Then behind and below us we could see the mysterious dark green crater which lay at the base of the precipitous crater walls that surrounded us and here and there odd bursts of steam jets filtered upwards through the foliage.

Grandfather was in high excitement. He hopped up and down on the Perceiver's horn and then gazed everywhere through his binoculars: up at the great expanse of sky, into the depths of the crater and across towards the lake ('Lake Naivasha…it must be!' he shouted)…all the while exhorting the Perceiver to look in this direction and that and to marvel with him at every sight. She nodded and turned and leaned from side to side. 'Yes…it has been worth coming up here. How beautiful it all is…how nice it is to see further than ever before.'

Meanwhile Kush dozed on her horn, his back turned away from us all. I had had enough of sightseeing and wanted to crawl down the crater a little way. I knew the Perceiver wouldn't be able to descend with her long legs and I had a suspicion that Grandfather would say a definite 'no!' if I asked him. So I quietly edged past the slumbering Kush and worked my way down the giraffe's neck, body and tail and onto the ground. It was quite easily done and

I was able to creep over the rim of the crater without being seen by any of them.

The part of crater I had landed on was even steeper than I expected and I had to hold firmly onto leaves and twigs as I climbed down. The ground was hot and slimy-black after the rains. I didn't like the feel of it at all. No, I decided firmly. This is no place for an adventure, even for the most intrepid of mice. So I turned back. Suddenly, the leaf I was holding came away and I began sliding and slithering rapidly down the steep slope towards one of these hot steam jets that burst upwards. I tried to grab onto bushes as I fell but I was going too fast. I was soon surrounded by pungent smelling steam and it seemed to embrace and enfold me like some miasmatic force, pulling me nearer and nearer to the abyss below. 'Grandfather!… Kush!…help!' I screamed. But how could they hear my plaintive little voice from so far away? I could no longer see ahead or behind me now as I plunged downwards. I even tried to curl my tail around rocks and the stunted trees that loomed suddenly before me and seemed so much a part of this nightmarish landscape, but they were too big and my tail too short and I skidded past. I screamed for help again but it was useless, there seemed to be no animal around to help or get help.

I must have been quite far down, because the steam was now much hotter and it hissed upwards and as I rolled downwards I could hear bubbling and gurgling noises. I had to stop! But what could I do? Just as I was about to give up all hope, I felt a powerful jerk and came to a sudden halt. I looked around and saw that my rucksack had got itself miraculously caught on a protruding branch. My legs swung wildly underneath as I tried to find a foothold, but I was too tired and I lay limply against the steamy foul-smelling earth, hoping that my rucksack would continue to hold me.

But that was not to be. There was a deafening crack and the branch gave way. Oh no! The dreadful downwards plunge had begun again. I was now almost at the bottom of the crater. Suddenly, I felt a dead weight on the tip of my tail. I jerked to another halt, my whiskers a hair's breadth away from the green slime. What on earth had stopped me this time?

Then I heard a cough. 'An unwise adventure my good friend of the many eyes.'

I swung round. It was the leopard! Never in my whole little life was I so happy to see the rather frightening face of a leopard. 'Oh, thank you! Thank you!' I wailed.

The leopard chuckled softly and curled his claws around my tail and then held me gently in his large paw.

'How did you know I was here?' I asked.

'Ah well, I was minding my own business as usual, when I heard a commotion at the rim of the crater. Your Grandfather was busy rushing about on the giraffe's back calling you, and that parrot was shrieking and flying in a frenzy, and the giraffe was pacing to and fro along the rim saying over and over again: "I wanted a surprise…

but not this kind of surprise…oh dear…oh dear." An odd thing to say under the circumstances, I thought to myself. But then there's no accounting for how animals behave in a crisis.'

The leopard sat back on his haunches and looked around him. 'I've never been down this far before. It's an unwelcome sort of a place and I don't like the look of those steam jets. Let's be pushing on then.' He placed me on his neck and started the difficult climb back to the others at the crater's edge. The going was hard. The leopard climbed and slipped back and climbed on again, digging his paws deeply into the soggy earth. He breathed rapidly in short bursts through clenched teeth.

We were still working our way upwards when, to our surprise, we came upon a long piece of climbing rope lying taut against the side of the crater. We followed it back downwards a few paces until we heard a voice drifting towards us through the mist.

'This rope has come to an end…what do I do now? Oh dear…oh dear.'

We climbed towards it and saw poor Grandfather dangling on the end of the rope. 'Livingstone! My dear boy…' he choked. Nothing more was said. The leopard helped him onto his neck and Grandfather pulled me roughly to his chest, holding me so tightly that I nearly stopped breathing altogether.

The leopard grasped the rope between his teeth and continued the climb. The rope took us straight back to one of the Perceiver's ankles, where Grandfather had cleverly tied its opposite end. The giraffe was peering here, there and everywhere while Kush hovered about her head repeating over and over: 'I'm going down! I'm going after them!'

'No!' We all shouted and the leopard gave the rope a pull. Kush took one look at the leopard and disappeared and the giraffe pulled back, her eyelashes fluttering wildly in alarm. She calmed a little when she saw him lift Grandfather and me gently off his neck and place us in the grass. The leopard cuffed my head softly before disappearing in the bush. Elusive as ever he didn't even give me a chance to say thank you or goodbye.

The Perceiver dropped her head down and nuzzled us both. 'I suppose I must thank you for giving me such a surprise…but did you have to put yourself at such risk to do it little fellow?'

'I hadn't intended to,' I replied. 'It was supposed to be a very ordinary little adventure.'

'Ah, now I remember what it was,' said the Perceiver.

'What what was?' I asked.

'What Hugill's last words were. He said that all perception had its limits and that I mustn't be surprised if in fact something as small and almost imperceptible as a mouse could give me the greatest of surprises. How amusing. I was so intent on looking farther than ever before that I never thought to look nearer than ever before.'

'Do you think he knew I'd go over the edge to explore?'

'Well, given Hugill's own perceptive abilities and his sheer wizardliness, I would say that he had an idea that the conjunction of a pair of intrepid exploring mice with a mysterious volcanic crater would provide the Perceiver with a surprise of some kind,' said Grandfather laughing.

We were back on the giraffe's horns. 'Mmmm...well now that I know what a genuine surprise really feels like, I'm not sure that I'm too keen on them.' Then she stood very still, gazing in the direction of the distant hills.

We remained in that position for quite some time before she broke it with a deep rich 'Ahhh...' which welled up from the base of her long neck. 'Ahhh,' she said again. 'He did say one more thing, that clever monkey friend of yours.'

'What?' asked Grandfather.

'He called us the "Ruminative Prophets of Africa." He said that giraffes were very lucky because we had the wisdom of foreknowledge, most of the time anyway! Perhaps he's right,' and she laughed and turned her back on the crater.

We found Kush hiding in a tree. He resumed his perch on the giraffe's horn without a shriek or a squawk and we continued on down the slope. By early evening we were back on the plain. The Perceiver made for a lonely acacia tree. She dropped us onto the land for a while so she could stretch her neck up and feed on the topmost leaves of the tree. We too indulged in a light snack, sitting comfortably near the Perceiver's legs.

On the horizon three more giraffes appeared, one behind the other like tall black sentinels. The Perceiver tore the leaves off one more branch and paced towards them. They immediately surrounded her, and all four of them put their heads together and conferred in buzzing whispers. At last she pulled away and turned back towards us.

'What was all that about?' shrieked Kush loudly.

'Hush…' she said. 'It seems my friends that a reception committee awaits us at the lake.' And she bent down to pick us all up for the walk towards Lake Naivasha.

CHAPTER EIGHT

"THE PAPYRUS-SEDGE SHORE"

We crossed the plain towards the shores of Lake Naivasha. As we did so we passed a troupe of baboons settling in a large acacia for the night. And dotted across the plain we could make out a herd of buffalo quietly grazing. At the lake's edge beds of long-stemmed papyrus rose and fell. Hugging the papyrus and dotted across the lake were immense flat stretches of lily-leaves, their white lotus flowers tightly closed for the night. As we drew near, we heard the most extraordinary sound. Blast! Swish! Grunt! It went.

'What was that? What was that?' asked Kush, ruffling his feathers and turning around on the Perceiver's horn.

The giraffe stopped and we listened.

It came again: 'Blast…swish…grunt…blast…swish… grunt…'

The Perceiver scrutinised the lake for some minutes and then said: 'It's our reception committee; over there in the mud, just beyond the reeds.'

We peered at the lake and in the dusk light managed to make out four dark humps just above the surface of the water. And then we saw four pairs of ears and four pairs of pink-rimmed eyes.

'Four hippopotami,' hissed Grandfather loudly

Four distinct grunts were emitted in reply. And then the largest of them said: 'I take it we are addressing our esteemed and wise friend Hugill Macauley's questing party?'

Kush immediately perked up at the sound of his dear friend's name. He flew down to a papyrus stem which bent over under his weight, placing him very near the four hippopotami. 'When did you see Hugill? When? When? When?' he asked, falling into repetitions in his excitement, the papyrus stem bounding rapidly up and down.

'Ah well...as to that I couldn't tell you,' said the hippopotamus.

'Surely you can remember if it was yesterday or the day before that, even last night?' said Kush, an hysterical shriek forming in the back of his throat.

The hippopotami became so entranced by the papyrus-stem rising up and down, inches away from their large noses, that it was a full minute before one of them replied: 'As to time…it is of no great consequence to any of us on this lake.'

Grandfather intervened at this point, before Kush's frenzied hopping and bobbing along the papyrus-stem caused these creatures offence. 'Could you not tell us how many lotus-flower openings and closings since you last saw our mutual friend?' he asked diplomatically.

A long silence followed and then one of them pushed her way forward shyly. 'I could tell you in great detail about the wondrous mechanism of the lotus-flowers which regulates all our lives on the lake. I could tell you about its exquisite scent and its colour: not quite white, not quite cream, a hint of lilac at its centre. But as to counting…why would we do that? What would we do with that kind of knowledge on this lake? Time passes, dusk falls, dawn breaks; we wade, we wallow, we roll and splash about. What more do we need?'

Kush leapt off the papyrus-stem in a huff and flew onto a lily-pod, turning his back on us all.

'Oh dear…have we given offence?' said yet another hippopotamus sadly, preparing to disappear back into the mud.

'You mustn't worry about Kush, his sulks never last long,' I said. 'But perhaps you have a message from Hugill?'

'Oh but we do, we do,' they all replied in unison, delighted it seemed to please us at last.

In a trice Kush was bouncing on the papyrus-stem again.

'He gave each one of us a line to remember,' said the largest hippopotamus.

'Which line came first?' asked Grandfather.

'Oh dear…I don't know…he did tell us, but I forgot now.' And the poor animal blushed a livid purple.

'We must know the sequence,' said Grandfather.

'Does sequence matter so very much?' asked the hippopotamus.

'Yes!' we all said.

'Oh dear…' and all four of them gazed sadly into each other's eyes and looked as if they were about to disappear into the mud again in silence.

Grandfather quickly reassured them that it didn't matter and that we would work it out somehow.

'Wait, wait…let me see if I can remember who was standing where when the lines were given,' said the large hippopotamus. And he began to stage manage the other three, first into one position and then another and another, the whole process taking an age on account of their bulk. There was much splashing and grunting and heaving, but at last the hippopotamus seemed satisfied. 'Yes, I think that's it. Now mine was most certainly first:

Go forth on two horns and a hump

and he beamed with delight after delivering his line. The second hippopotamus pushed forward and spoke:

To the forbidden sanctuary of the pink plumage

And there was much grunting and nodding and agreeing. Then came the third hippopotamus:

There to find one sadly misnamed

More nodding and grunting followed.

And then the fourth hippopotamus huffed and puffed in front of the others, causing a chop in the water about her:

A bearer of peace who lives out of time and out of place

and she shook with delight.

The four hippopotami turned to face each other and grunted with deep satisfaction before sinking back into the mud, there to indulge further in their wallow and splurge.

'Well, that's the limit!' shrieked Kush, bouncing up and down on his papyrus-stem.

'I do admit that Hugill is being a trifle obscure,' said Grandfather writing the message down in his notebook. 'Have you any ideas Perceiver?'

'All I know is that I have two horns and a hump and therefore I have to take you somewhere. But where this *forbidden sanctuary* is I can't say. Let's sleep on it, perhaps we'll think more clearly in the morning.'

'Yes, I think you've got a point. I must say I am delighted you will still be with us. Would you mind lowering your head, I have a mind to sleep on a lotus leaf for the night? Come on Livingstone.'

The Perceiver complied and we clambered off and made for a bed of lotus leaves neatly tucked away amongst the tall papyrus grasses. I lay curled behind Grandfather. The lotus leaf trembled on its liquid surface. A lotus-flower rocked gently nearby, its enfolded promises hidden away until morning.

CHAPTER NINE

A CLUE FROM THE LOTUS WORLD

It was the smell. Yes. It was most certainly the smell: of sweet nectar and honey; of rosewater and julep. I opened my eyes and found myself gazing directly into the creamy-lilac eye of a lotus flower. It must be morning. I looked round, Grandfather was still asleep; the Perceiver and Kush were nowhere to be seen. I resumed my contemplation of the flower.

Suddenly there was a violent commotion beneath us. The lotus leaf rocked wildly and we began to roll alarmingly near to its edge. It was a log! As if from nowhere it had appeared out of the water to carry us away with it. By now Grandfather was awake, hopping up and down on the log.

'Livingstone, what's happening?'

'We're on a log and its floating out into the centre of the lake!'

We walked gingerly from one end of its slimy, rippled surface to the other, trying to find a way to steer it towards the papyrus-sedge shore. But it seemed to be carried by some internal mechanism of its own because it drifted determinedly towards the centre of the lake.

Our predicament caused quite a sensation amongst the birdlife: a huge fish-eagle swooped low over us, a deep frown etching his black-eyes; two starlings hopped above us in frenzy; a heron dashed into a clump of papyrus and a kingfisher made repeated dives towards the log, its red beak snapping and clicking in alarm. At length it hovered near, saying softly: 'You do realise that you're riding on the back of the only crocodile on the lake!'

'What?' we both screamed in horror, looking more closely at the green-brown surface.

'I'll see if I can get help,' shouted the kingfisher, darting off towards some papyrus.

Meanwhile we huddled together, terrified lest the crocodile became suspicious of our presence. The kingfisher returned at last to inform us that help was on its way and that we were not to move from our position.

Fortunately we didn't have to wait too long before two large frogs leapt out of the water and onto the crocodile's back. 'Take a deep breath and hold on tight,' they said. We climbed onto their backs and held on as they dived into the lake. White bubbles flew around us chaotically and then all was calm as we slowly descended into the murky green underworld of the lake, surrounded by silence and watched, wide-eyed, by oddly shaped fish, which darted near and darted quickly away. We were carried through a forest thick with papyrus-stem and sedge which drifted this way and that above its muddy anchorage, to emerge finally amongst a bed of lotus leaves. The frogs deposited us on a large leaf, where we lay gasping for breath.

When we recovered we pulled all the contents from our rucksacks and spread them across the flat leaves to dry out in the sun. A family of lily-trotters offered to act as weights on our damp maps. Meanwhile, we investigated the contents of our ration boxes. All was well. They at least were still dry. So we were able to offer the lotus-dwellers a light snack in repayment for all their exertions on our behalf. They gathered round, fascinated by the dried sausage and the biscuits.

Grandfather and I stretched out in the sun, our heads cushioned by lotus-flowers. The kingfisher wrestled with a piece of sausage, the lily-trotter family and frogs shared a few biscuits, while the two of us drowsed and dreamed, engulfed by rich and hypnotic aromas.

A noise startled me. I opened my eyes. Something very peculiar was happening. The kingfisher's red beak had grown long and had developed enormous sharp white teeth. He was snapping them at me over and over again. The frogs had developed horns, three horns each and they were coming nearer and nearer, their funny arms stretched out and a sneer on their faces. The lily-trotters had disappeared and in their place were lots of white paper balls with writing on them.

My voice felt thick and heavy as I screamed for help. I tried to run away, but an invisible web held me down. The frogs and the kingfisher came closer and I pressed my head further back into the lotus-flower. Just as they were about to pounce, I fell. Down, down, down I plunged to the very bottom of the lake. I rolled and rolled in the squelchy brown mud. Sleep, I thought. Yes, I'll just lie in the mud and sleep and maybe it will all go away. Just then something pushed its way through the mud. First a beak appeared followed by a long sinuous neck and then the body of a fish, a fish covered in pink feathers.

'How odd meeting you here,' said the fish.

'Well I can say the same about you,' I replied.

'Oh no,' said the fish. 'I'm in the right place. I belong here, but you don't.'

'Why?'

'Why? Because I belong in your dream, you don't.'

'I don't understand,' I said, rolling around in the mud.

The fish sighed. 'Well silly, you're supposed to be dreaming your dream, not acting in it. Who's dreaming it for you then, your Grandfather?'

I began to wish I hadn't replied to the fish at all. 'Perhaps I left my dream behind in the lotus-flower and this is all real?' I said, trembling now from whisker to tail.

'Mmmm,' mused the fish. 'Could be, but then I know I'm not real. You see, who's ever heard of a fish with feathers on it? Do you see what I mean?'

'Yes…yes I see. Then perhaps I've left the real world altogether and have become another dream,' I replied.

'Oh no,' cackled the fish. 'What an illogical little fellow you are. If you ceased to exist and had just become another dream, then I too would cease to exist as your dream. Do you see?'

I didn't, but I sighed with relief at the fish's absolute conviction that I must exist somewhere. 'Could we change the subject?' I asked.

'It's entirely up to you,' replied the fish.

'Have you any idea what kind of bird your bird part is?'

'I don't know. You must know the answer to that question, you created me.'

'Oh.'

Since anything I said was going to lead to confusion, I lay back in the warm mud and thought very deeply. The fish meanwhile hovered over me, every now and then dipping its beak into the mud.

'Strange thing,' it said, pulling an empty beak out of the mud and breaking the long silence between us. 'I can never seem to find the right kind of food in this lake, for my bird-part that is. As a fish it's quite habitable, but as a bird I do feel misplaced here.'

I immediately perked up at this. 'Where would you rather be?' I asked.

'Oh you should know that,' replied the fish.

I thought again in silence. 'Well, as a bird you clearly wish to belong to another lake, a different kind of lake to this one. You know, other birds live here quite happily.'

'Mmm...I don't like it...it's, it's, well it's too fresh for me. I like my water to have a taste, to have a bit of a fizz.'

'If I could just wake up, then I might be able to solve your problem for you,' I answered.

The fish cackled again. 'Perhaps if I were to bury myself in the mud again, you might be able to take charge of your dream. It certainly seems to have got out of control.' And the fish (or was it a bird?) disappeared into the mud.

Oh dear, how was I to get back to the lotus-flower? I rolled around in the mud and then I saw a papyrus-stem floating towards me. I grabbed onto it and started to climb to the surface of the lake. But as I climbed, I felt as if my tail was being pulled.

'Ouch!' I shouted. 'Stop pulling...stop it...leave me alone...'

'Livingstone, wake up! Wake up!'

I opened my eyes. It was Grandfather and he was pulling my tail.

'Oh Grandfather, don't tell me you're in the mud with me!' I wailed. 'I had hoped you were still on the lotus leaf and could pull me out of it.'

'Livingstone, what are you talking about? What mud? I am still on the lotus leaf.'

'I met this fish-bird ...and the bird-part can't live in the lake.'

'Fish-bird? Oh wake up, dear boy, we're all still here.'

I sat up and looked around. The kingfisher was still wrestling with the same bit of sausage, its beak back to normal. There were no paper balls. The lily-trotters and frogs were finishing their biscuits.

'Grandfather I must tell you my dream. Please let me…it did disturb me so,' I pleaded.

'Of course my dear boy,' he said, pulling my tail fondly.

The others drew near and I told them of the strange conversation I had had with the fish-bird.

'Extraordinary!' said one of the frogs, rubbing the top of its head to make sure there were no horns.

'It's a jumble of Hugill's message, but perhaps there's something in it,' Grandfather mused and then he turned to the others. 'Are there any other kinds of lakes for birds?'

The kingfisher shrugged. 'Well you could have been dreaming about the soda lakes, South of here. But we don't go there. I don't think you'll find any birds or fish there, not our kind anyway. But you could try them.'

'Mmmm…Hugill did say *a forbidden sanctuary* perhaps that's where he meant. As you say, it's worth a try,' and he pulled one of his maps towards him and studied it. 'Yes, I see them. And look Livingstone the Southernmost lake takes us across the border into Tanzania! Hugill is taking us to Tanzania! I wonder why?'

I felt rather pleased with my morning's work. But I studiously avoided any contact with the lotus-flower. I had the distinct feeling that it had something to do with my dream, especially, when I noticed, in the corner of my eye, that it was unmistakeably winking at me.

CHAPTER TEN

GOING SOUTH

'Before we go I must ask the kingfisher about the crocodile,' said Grandfather and taking out his notebook he asked the bird why it was the only crocodile on the lake.

'Well, the temperature is not right for them in this lake, but he just appeared a while back and settled in.'

'Mmm...perhaps an evolved crocodile,' mused Grandfather, noting it all down. And when he had finished he said: 'Everything is now quite dry. I think it's time to get back to land,' and he helped me to repack my rucksack.

We parted company from the kingfisher and lily-trotters and the frogs guided us along from lily bed to lily bed until we regained the lake's edge. The Perceiver and Kush were there waiting for us.

'Guess what? Guess what? Guess what?' shrieked Kush excitedly, bobbing up and down on the giraffe's horn.

'You're bound to tell us, so I won't guess,' I said laughing as the giraffe lowered her head for us to climb on.

'We know where we're heading,' said Kush triumphantly.

'Where?' Grandfather asked.

'South…to the soda lakes,' he replied.

Grandfather and I looked at each other in astonishment. 'I know,' I said simply.

'You know…how do you know?'

'I had a dream in a lotus flower and in the dream I was given a clue about them.'

'Oh stuff and nonsense! Who believes in dreams? We know for certain, don't we Giraffe?'

'Mmm,' she replied. 'But I do believe in dreams too.'

'Humph,' was all that came from Kush.

The Perceiver continued: 'I had a word with some giraffe cousins who have just journeyed from the South. They suggested that we try the two soda lakes to the South. They also said that they had heard tell of a strange bird that lives on them. But they weren't at all sure.'

I looked at Grandfather, who put a paw to his mouth: dreams were sacred things, as were the secrets they contained.

We said farewell to the frogs and set off South along the Eastern wall of the great Rift. The route took us into a luscious green valley of acacia forest interlaced with grassy clearings and rivulets.

We paced along in companionable silence for some hours. When the sun had reached its highest point and the heat became too intense for travel, we decided to take a break. The Perceiver made for a large clump of acacias beside a river. She placed us neatly on a hollow log close to the river's edge and paced off towards the largest of the trees, where she nibbled at the luscious top leaves.

Yet even at the river's edge there seemed to be no relief from the midday heat. I decided to explore the inside of the log. It smelled of decayed leaves and damp wood, but it was at least cool: a dark stuffy kind of coolness. I called to Grandfather and Kush and they joined me at the opening. We made a comfortable bed out of the drier leaves and settled down to while away that part of the day.

Boredom soon set in. I looked down the length of the log. At first it was all so dark that I couldn't make anything out. Gradually my eyes became accustomed to the gloom and halfway along I saw what looked like a thick lace curtain. Fearing that it was yet another one of my strange dreams about to begin, I pointed it out to Grandfather.

'Let's go and investigate,' he said.

We crept closer to the curtain.

'Don't come any closer! Don't come any closer!' came a tiny voice from somewhere inside the curtain. We advanced further and discovered that it was a cobweb: an intricately woven web of white silken thread, the pattern quite unlike anything I had ever seen before. And at its centre was suspended a large black female spider.

'I've worked on this web for months!' she said, fixing us with all of her eight eyes. 'That stupid, clumsy old mongoose came crashing in here the other day and tore one end of it to shreds. I wish he would leave this log alone. I keep telling him that it has belonged to my family for centuries; "time out of mind" were my very words, but he wouldn't listen of course. "Share the log," he said. Share the log! How preposterous! I'm an artist and I need all this space to myself otherwise how am I to create my beautiful webs? Besides, as I told the mongoose, this isn't the only log in Africa. There must be hundreds of them all over the continent and it's such a small, insignificant one too. Anyway, what do you think of my latest creation?' and all of her eyes became lost in admiration of her handwork.

'It's beautiful,' we all agreed.

'Oh I know that! But is that all you can see?'

We looked more closely at the elaborate intertwinings, knottings and cross-lacings.

'Yes…except that it is the most complicated web I've yet come across. Should it tell us something?' asked Grandfather.

The spider looked very disappointed at this reply. 'Well, I must say, how very unobservant of you. I had another visitor a while back, during the great storm and he grasped it immediately. He looked closely at my web and said, "That's brilliant! It's a beginning without an end: the beginning gets swallowed up in the ending which gets swallowed up in the beginning, how wonderful." Those were his very words. He even asked me how long I had been busy on it because apparently it's mathematically impossible on a flat surface, you know.'

'Your visitor wasn't a monkey perhaps?' asked Grandfather.

'What if it was? At least he understood,' she replied disdainfully.

Grandfather moved a little closer and examined the web. He took off his rucksack and rummaged inside for a notebook and pencil. Then, using my magnifying glass, he worked his way along the web, taking notes and writing out equations and performing calculations all the while. 'Mmmm...Hugill's right. It looks like a kind of bottle twisted in on itself so that its bottom is also its top. There's no name for it because it hasn't been discovered yet. Remarkable, truly remarkable,' he breathed.

He returned to his notebook again and began drawing away busily, chewing the end of his pencil. Then, in desperation, he flung book and pencil to the floor of the log and paced up and down in front of the web. At length he put his paws to his eyes. 'I...I can't look at it any more... it's making me too dizzy. How long did it take you?'

'This one took me months, but I've been trying to do it on and off for years.'

'Absurd, I think it's absurd!' shrieked Kush, who had by now joined us.

'Why?' asked the spider, clearly amazed that anyone should call such artistic perfection absurd.

'What's the good of going to all this trouble in the dark? Absurd...absurd... absurd,' he replied.

The spider looked questioningly at Grandfather, who said apologetically, 'what Kush means is that perhaps you should construct your beautiful works where everyone can see and enjoy them.'

'To be torn to pieces by wind and rain! Elephant's tusks! Giraffe tongues! A Rhinoceros horn! How could you even think of it?' she cried, fixing her eyes on Kush.

'Well, I think it's a silly sort of life. If you're so good at making webs, you could fix them as quickly as you made them,' continued Kush doggedly.

'But what about my latest work, I can only do it in this log?'

'You can't surely live inside that particular web forever?' I asked her.

The poor little spider's world had been turned upside down, inside out and stretched to breaking point. Eight tears ran down her fat shiny black sides. 'The monkey understood everything,' she sniffed, 'all the hard work and the ingenuity. It is a stuffy sort of life and I know there's a whole world out there. But I am quite happy here. This is what I can do best and if it only gets recognised once in a long while…it doesn't matter…you see I know it's good,' and more tears ran down, wetting the web so that it twinkled and shone in the gloom.

Grandfather went up to her and whispered, his own voice rather hoarse, 'I understand you perfectly…,' and he gathered his pencil and notebook and turned away.

We waved goodbye and walked to the opening of the log. A tiny echo followed us from its dark depths: 'Come back again one day…'

We emerged into the sunlight once again and Grandfather sighed, looking back at the log: 'A rare and true artist Livingstone, and yet another of Hugill's unexpected treasures,' and we rejoined the Perceiver.

'At least we know we're going in the right direction,' said Kush. 'Hugill was here before us, and not so long ago.'

'Oh Kush, well done…,' said Grandfather, his voice seeming to come from far off, still entranced after the encounter with the spider.

We clambered back onto the Perceiver's head and continued our journey, following the water-course for some hours before changing direction and moving further along the Eastern edge of the valley. After some hours I noticed that the Perceiver's mood had changed. She stopped often to listen to the jumble of animal noises which surrounded us, her ears turned sharply in every direction and her eyes moving rapidly this way and that. She kept looking behind her too and once she climbed a small hill to gaze up the length and breadth of the valley. We varied our course regularly: now pacing through forest, now along river, now across plain; a zigzag pattern, back and forth across the valley. And with each change in direction the Perceiver listened.

'Is anything the matter?' I whispered once, leaning over to her one ear. She just shook her head. When night fell I noticed that her watchfulness increased, her surveillance of the valley intensified. And while Grandfather and Kush were rocked to sleep by her rhythmical pacing, I maintained watch with her. With the coming of the dawn her tensed neck relaxed, but only slightly and a sigh rippled up from its base. Nothing was said between us, but we both continued to listen and to watch. We breakfasted and journeyed on; rested at midday and journeyed on again. By now Grandfather and Kush had sensed her concern. The tension increased between us all and Kush never left the safety of her horn but stayed close. Grandfather constantly surveyed the valley with his binoculars. Not that he, or any of us knew what perturbed the Perceiver so.

Towards late afternoon we reached a wide, deep pool. And there, gazing intently into the water was a young rhinoceros. He immediately picked up his ears as we approached and turned towards us, sniffing and snorting, his horns thrusting at the air above him. His leathery skin lay in broad wrinkles and creases around his powerful shoulders and was covered in dried mud and bits of grass. A flattened area of grass nearby indicated that a satisfying roll had recently been indulged in.

The rhinoceros had clearly not been the source of the Perceiver's deep disquiet, for she ambled straight past and made for the pool. Once there she deposited us on the grass and stretched her long legs out, she bent her elegant head into the water for a long drink.

Meanwhile the rhinoceros had returned to gaze at his reflection in the pool, turning his head this way and that, as if to gain a better view of his two horns.

'What are you looking at?' I asked politely.

The rhinoceros lifted his head a touch and sniffed at me, his crumpled and puckered nostrils flaring all the time. When, at length, he decided that I was posing no threat to his bit of the pool, he said: 'Myself.'

'Why?'

The rhinoceros snorted and looked back at himself in the water and then at me again. 'I have a problem with my horns,' he said shortly.

'What problem?'

'They're always in my way. I can't see beyond them to see exactly what I look like. No matter which way I turn or at what angle I rotate my head, it comes back to the same thing every time: my horns are in the way.'

He turned dejectedly back to his reflection. I watched him gazing at himself for some time then I had an idea. 'You don't think that the problem has something to do with the position of your eyes?'

The rhinoceros looked up and frowned. 'My eyes?'

'Yes,' I said. 'They're too far apart and on the sides of your head. This means that however hard you try to see your whole face in the water you won't succeed. Of course, if they were set higher up in your forehead then you'd be able to see your whole face all in one.'

The rhinoceros snorted in reply.

'But,' I continued reassuringly, 'you can use each eye to get a complete view of each of your two profiles; put the two together and you can then picture your entire face in your mind.'

The rhinoceros gazed at me in wonder. And then slowly, very slowly, his large fleshy lips curled into a beatific smile. He returned his gaze to the pool again, quite content to look lovingly at each of his two profiles.

'Come on Livingstone,' shouted Grandfather, as he settled back on the Perceiver's horn, having refilled our water bottles. I waved goodbye at the one eye facing me, but the rhinoceros never shifted his gaze from the pool.

The Perceiver increased her speed, now quite overt in her glances behind and her quick changes of direction. Ahead of us lay a small hillock. Upon reaching it, she climbed up and gazed back in the direction we had just come. And then she inclined her head towards a rocky outcrop about half a mile away, on the Western side of the valley. There, sitting on top, was the biggest lion I had ever seen. His short-cropped golden-brown mane gathered in great thick wedges around his head and he was growling, his huge fanged mouth wide open in a ghastly grimace. He stretched a powerful paw out menacingly, as if to grab at us.

We must make haste,' whispered the Perceiver. She turned her back on the lion and descended the hill at a gallop. I looked around and saw that the lion had already left the rocky outcrop. I laced my tail around her hump and held on tightly. Grandfather did the same and Kush slipped off her horn and into the soft tufted nook below it. Thus safely positioned for the dreadful chase, all that we could do now was to encourage her along.

CHAPTER ELEVEN
THE CHASE

The Perceiver galloped into the night. The darkened forms of acacia trees loomed large and then fell away. The stars rose and fell above us, as if they too were being chased, but across the great expanse of black sky; brilliant partners in our race towards the horizon where an ochre tinge lapped at the land's edge. Once, our path was blocked by a herd of buffalo making their way unhurried across the valley. As one they turned to survey us in their bemused and slow fashion, their arched horns silhouetted against the sky, surprised at our frantic hurry on such a calm night. We followed a shallow water-course for some miles before our path was again blocked, this time by a lonely elephant quietly hosing down its vast hulk with jets of water from its trunk. The valley was continuing its animal activities, our desperate flight an incidental moment in a long African night.

We climbed a high rocky outcrop which gave an unimpeded view behind us. The Perceiver stood very still, listening and watching. An unmistakable growl was heard from the West. We turned towards the noise and there, in a clearing, stood the lion, his yellow eyes staring straight at us, his powerful body poised for the chase.

'Oh no! no! no!' shrieked Kush. 'I'm tired of all this galloping…is there nowhere to hide at all?…at all?…at all?' and fear gave way to repetition as Kush turned round and round on the Perceiver's head.

'No my friend,' she sighed.

Grandfather rummaged in his rucksack and pulled out two of his restorative wholemeal biscuits and a square of chocolate.

'Put your tongue out Perceiver, these will restore some energy.'

She received these small offerings with a grateful inclination of her head and descended the outcrop.

Towards dawn a soft mist settled on the land. The Perceiver slowed down and finally stopped altogether, her exhausted body trembling all over and her breathing strained and coming in sharp hoarse bursts. I noticed too that she held her jaws tightly closed as if to hold back as much air as she could. She picked her way through the mist, at times lifting her head to see above and over it. A few yards away and clearly discernible above the mist was a dense thicket. We walked into it, the Perceiver burying herself deeply in the bush. She leant her whole weight against a tree and her eyelids fluttered once or twice and then closed, though her ears maintained their alertness, twisting round constantly.

With the mist calm descended. Animal noises filtered our way thickly, as if from a great distance.

'Livingstone, Kush, we'll take it in turns to sleep. You two have yours now and I'll keep watch,' Grandfather commanded. We both obeyed and sleep overcame us instantly.

A few minutes later, or so it seemed, Grandfather was pulling my tail. 'Livingstone! Livingstone! Wake up!'

I groaned and tried to pull away. 'But I've only been asleep for a few minutes,' I wailed.

'No you haven't, you've been asleep for an hour, now it's my turn,' he said, settling back and shutting his eyes.

I felt rather frightened, maintaining watch on my own, so I called to Kush softly. But he turned his back on me and feigned not to hear. I peered through the damp cold mist. It was beginning to lift slightly and a green-blue sky was just visible in patches.

Suddenly two giraffes appeared from nowhere. I tapped the Perceiver on the nose, but she was already awake. The other two immediately surrounded her and they began to confer in soft whispers and buzzes. Grandfather and Kush stirred reluctantly, and we tried to hear what they were saying. At length they pulled away and disappeared into the mist, as quietly as they had come.

'What is it? What is it?' asked Kush excitedly.

'Our hunter is still hunting. He is stalking us on the edge of this forest,' replied the Perceiver with a weary sigh.

'Eek!' shrieked Kush.

'Is he really that close?' asked Grandfather.

'Yes.'

'Why us? Why not the others as well?'

'It seems that he has chosen us.'

'What do we do now?' I asked.

'We'll give him the slip in this mist. I have an idea,' she said, setting off again.

Her route out of the forest was in the direction we had come earlier and in the path of the lion. She moved very quietly, the moist ground absorbing her hoof-falls. She picked her way delicately around trees and bush, avoiding the sharp branches and twigs. Once she stopped to listen and we heard a muffled growl. We stayed very still for some time before moving on again. Then we saw his big brown body gliding slowly past in the opposite direction. He hadn't seen us as we were safely hidden behind a large tree and downwind of him. After some minutes of painful stillness the giraffe pressed on Northwards and out of the forest. Using the mist for cover she circled the edge of the forest and worked her way South again, moving as quickly as she could.

'Well done, Perceiver!' whispered Grandfather.

'We're not clear of him yet,' she replied.

When the mist finally cleared, we found ourselves in the middle of an open plain at the base of the Eastern valley wall. The giraffe hastily surveyed the terrain and was about to pace rapidly across it when Grandfather, binoculars aloft, called to her urgently: 'Quick! Look over there!' We looked in the direction he was pointing. Buried in the long yellow grass with only his huge head visible was the lion. He was grinning at us, his eyes narrowed to thin slits. Then he sat up and waved his powerful paw at us again. The Perceiver shuddered and galloped away across the plain. The lion seemed to growl in frustration before beginning his chase yet again.

On and on we galloped. Mile upon mile of scrub-land fell away underfoot. Grandfather kept a close watch on our rear through his binoculars, reporting every sighting of the lion. At first he nearly closed the gap between us, then he fell away and disappeared altogether for some time only to reappear again, parallel with us, though some distance away. At last the Perceiver could go no further; gasping for breath, her long neck shuddering with effort, she came to a stop. Ahead was an extensive jumble of grey boulders piled massively on top of each other and lying in heaps at the base, with bush and the odd small tree sprouting from a crevice. The Perceiver worked her way round it until she found a shady area. Here, in the cool, she rested before what must be the final onslaught between her and the lion.

'Ah…ah…ahhhh…,' laughed the lion from a boulder above us. It was a rich and deep voice emanating from a red cavern of a mouth and from between sharp white teeth. The giraffe held herself upright and pulled back.

'You can't escape me you know,' and the lion threw back his large head and bellowed, banging his chest with a large forepaw. 'But I enjoyed the chase all the same, haven't had such a run for my money in years.' And he bowed his head in thanks. 'Well, now that I have you all in my clutches, so to speak, we can have a proper chat.' And he leapt regally from boulder to boulder to the ground, landing about six feet away.

The Perceiver reared back.

'Oh no,' said the lion in a bored tone, waving his large paw at the giraffe. 'Don't start galloping again…there are limits to this game…and it is nearing midday you know, far too hot to go dashing about. As I was about to say, I do have a…' but before he could finish his sentence the Perceiver reared up, her fur bristling all over. The lion, now dangerously close to her legs, sat back on his haunches, and lifted his paws protectively. Seconds later the giraffe gave him a resounding kick on the shoulder. A look of confusion mingled with intense pain crossed his face. He shook his large head, rubbed his shoulder with a paw and limped off mumbling: 'She's got no sense that lady…no sense at all. I can't understand her…I just can't.'

The Perceiver sighed a deep and satisfying sigh. 'Elderly I might be, but I haven't lost my touch yet. We won't have any more trouble from him now, nor any lion for that matter. He'll advise all his friends to steer clear of us.'

'Well that's a relief. Mind you, I don't dislike them as much as I do leopards,' said Kush, sounding most brave now that the lion had retreated.

'Why is that?' I asked.

'Oh, that's because lions are such lazy creatures. They sleep twenty-one hours out of twenty-four, which means that at least I stand some chance of getting away. But leopards…I never know where I am with them. They can creep up on one at any time…' and he shuddered, flapping his wings.

'Thank you Perceiver, for placing yourself at such a risk on our behalf,' said Grandfather.

The giraffe merely inclined her head ever so slightly.

We continued our journey through a valley that had become less threatening now that our long-awaited enemy had been so summarily dealt with.

'All the same,' said Grandfather after we had covered a few more miles. 'There was something rather odd about his face.'

'What do you mean Grandfather?' I asked.

'Mmmmm…it seemed to me as though he wasn't actually chasing us at all. The chase became a game, of course. I realise that. But when it was all over I think he had a different intent in mind.'

'What makes you think that?'

'Well he looked so confused at the end of it all.'

The giraffe laughed softly. 'Don't be fooled. Lions play all the time. Everything's a game to them, even the hunt to kill.'

'Perhaps you're right,' replied Grandfather, still frowning deeply. 'But I am not entirely satisfied. There was something odd about him…if only I can put my paw on it.' And he went very silent, gazing straight ahead.

'I'm bored stiff on this horn!' said Kush, preparing to take off. 'I think I'll fly ahead for a while and see how far South those soda lakes are.' And he disappeared in a flurry of green feathers and shrieks and laughs.

'I hope he doesn't get lost,' I said to the giraffe.

'Oh there's not much chance of that in this valley. Besides he must exercise his wings and give my poor horn a rest. His talons are rather sharp, particularly when he gets excited.'

Grandfather and I laughed at this. 'Dear Kush,' said Grandfather

Some hours later a luminous green ball of feathers came hurtling out of the sky and Kush landed on the Perceiver's horn in a state of confusion, his wings flapping wildly.

'What is it? What is it?' asked Grandfather, trying to calm the parrot down.

'It's dreadful, that's what it is! simply dreadful!'

'What is?' we all asked in alarm.

'I've seen it! I've actually seen it and it's ghastly…' shrieked Kush, not even hearing us.

'What Kush? What?' persisted Grandfather.

'The lake…the soda lake,' he replied at last, shutting his eyes tightly, as if to ward off the memory.

'Oh dear…' was all that the Perceiver said and she slowed down a touch, perhaps delaying our inevitable arrival at the soda lake.

CHAPTER TWELVE

"OUT OF TIME AND OUT OF PLACE"

The valley began to widen. The terrain became flatter and sparser. The horizon ahead shimmered white and a startling pink. What stretched before us was the first of the formidable soda lakes. Its acrid-alkaline waters were covered here and there in soda flats which glistened pink and white in the intense heat; in odd places these had crumbled and broken, like an eerie moonscape which had unexpectedly found itself on earth. And there were hot springs that burst out in jets from rocks at the edge of the lake

The soda lake was edged by a dusty plain dotted with dull green bush and the odd acacia tree. The Perceiver walked towards the largest of the trees which grew directly beside the lake. She deposited us on the dry grass and sought what shelter she could under sparsely covered branches. The three of us walked towards a soda flat. We picked our way gingerly across its hot surface for a few feet before Kush rose into the air squawking frantically,

'I don't like this at all! at all!' and flew back to the giraffe. We were not far behind, relieved to feel the grass and dust beneath us.

We set up camp beneath the tree. I grabbed at my water bottle, intending to take a long drink, when I felt a restraining paw.

'We must conserve our small supply, Livingstone,' said Grandfather gently. 'There will be no refilling of these bottles for quite some time.'

I obeyed and took a small sip, aching for more. We shared a biscuit and a piece of sausage but it was too hot to eat and none of us finished our share. We slept fitfully in the white-hot glare coming off the lake. Towards late afternoon the glare at last subsided. The pinks of the soda crystals were transmuted now to a dull orange, here and there a hint of gold shining through.

'Grandfather, how are we going to cross this lake?' I asked.

'I don't know Livingstone, I just don't know,' he sighed.

'I wish I could help you my friends,' said the Perceiver, 'but my part in your adventure ends here. I have no way of crossing this lake.'

'Thank you Perceiver. And may I say how sorry we all are that you will not be continuing further with us,' said Grandfather.

'Ah well as to that…' but she forbore to continue and looked mysteriously away.

Meanwhile, Kush raced up and down the branch above us in boredom and frustration, jerking his head in and out and in and out. 'Hugill's not getting me to fly across this lake…no sir! I draw the line right here!' and he drew an imaginary line in the air with his beak.

Suddenly there was a violent commotion at the very top of the tree. The topmost branches began to sway wildly and the leaves shivered furiously. Something was falling. We peered into the foliage and saw a huge brown object crashing and bumping its way down from branch to branch. 'Oops! Ouch! Oops!' came a desperate voice from within the mass of brown. At last it broke through the lowest layer of leaves and landed with a loud thud between Grandfather and me. We leapt back in alarm and stared at a big round ball of black and brown feathers. It rolled around heavily for a few minutes and then stopped. Everything went very silent as we waited to see what the strange creature would do next.

First a large wing stretched out tentatively. Then another. A brown head followed. The whole then lifted onto two pink-thin, bristle-haired legs and proceeded to sway dangerously. 'Oh dear…oh dear…I must have fallen asleep again. It's on account of all this waiting…oh dear… you've been so long in coming,' croaked a voice from an ancient cracked beak.

'Warrior!' shouted Grandfather and I in delight.

Kush immediately flew down to Warrior to prop him up after his great fall. The Perceiver bent her head down to sniff the old eagle inquisitively.

'How long have you been waiting in this tree?' Grandfather asked.

'Weeks! As soon as I returned to Africa, after giving you the message, Hugill said, "Warrior, go and wait in the large acacia tree beside the first soda lake." I came immediately and a desperate time I've had of it I can tell you, what with falling asleep so often and worrying I might miss you and having to search for food in this forsaken place.'

And he gathered himself up, tucking a few straying feathers neatly into his side and puffing out his chest.

Grandfather first introduced him to a bemused Perceiver and then offered him some restorative wholemeal biscuits. The old bird bowed graciously at the giraffe and then ate voraciously, snapping his beak with pleasure at each mouthful. 'Thank you Darwin, thank you. That feels much, much better…quite ready to face the future now, I think.'

'What future? What future?' shrieked Kush turning his back firmly on the soda lake.

'Ah now…,' said the old eagle nodding his head slowly.

We all crept a little nearer to hear what he was about to say next. He bent his head low and rocked gently back and forth on his talons. Whatever it was that caused him to ponder his words so deeply, it had to be of grave importance. Grandfather motioned us to complete silence, fearing that we'd jumble the old bird's thoughts. So we waited in silence for some minutes, our heads bent towards the eagle's beak. The rocking motion continued and the eagle's beak remained tightly shut.

'Grandfather, I think Warrior's asleep. In fact I'm sure he is,' I whispered.

Grandfather peered closely at the eagle's eyelids. They were firmly shut.

'Oh no! You're right Livingstone. Perhaps that's what Hugill meant by *one misnamed: a bearer of peace who lives out of time and out of place.* He does seem to spend most of his life in a timeless world of his own.'

The eagle jerked awake suddenly. 'Er…what was that? What's that you said? Space? Out into space? No…no my friends, I can't take you into space that's too far, even for my powerful wings. Besides that's not the simplest solution to our problem.'

'We weren't actually speaking about "space" but "place," but never mind that. What problem faces us Warrior?' asked Grandfather tentatively.

'Why I told you! The problem of flying over these lakes.'

'What!' shrieked Kush, 'are you telling us that you are going to fly us over these lakes?'

'But…but I've just told you,' said the eagle blankly, looking at our confused faces. 'Or…or have I been sleeping? Oh dear, one loses such faith in self at times,' and he sniffed hopelessly and turned away.

'Never mind! Never mind! Just don't fall asleep on the job that's all,' said Kush brusquely.

The eagle pulled himself up tall until he towered over Kush, who backed away slightly. 'Hugill would never have appointed me to the job if he thought I wasn't up to it,' he said, looking both defensive and ridiculously noble at the same time.

Meanwhile the Perceiver, who had listened to this entire interchange with a look of increasing concern, motioned to Grandfather. They walked to the edge of the shade where the giraffe lowered her head down to him and they conferred in buzzing whispers. Grandfather returned to us, a mischievous smile on his face.

'Warrior my good friend, is there perhaps one smell on earth which you cannot abide?'

The eagle thought for a while. 'The smell of winter,' he said at last, shivering at the very idea of it.

'Mmm,' said Grandfather, turning to the Perceiver.

She merely inclined her head saying, 'Leave it to me and I'll see what I can do,' and strolled back up the valley.

Before Kush and I could ask him what it was all about, Grandfather put his paw to his mouth. Then he approached Warrior again. 'When had you in mind departing?'

'Tomorrow. Mid-morning.'

'But....but it's too hot then!' wailed Kush. 'Why not do the journey at night?'

'Can't be done at night. Lose my bearings at night. Must be able to see the lake and the sky at all times,' replied Warrior stolidly.

'Yes, you've got a point,' said Grandfather. 'Well, we have a long day ahead. I think a good night's sleep is in order.'

Before Grandfather had even finished his sentence Warrior's eyelids had closed firmly for the night, his one leg tucked away behind his wing. The three of us settled down too. The soda lake had turned a ghostly green in the moonlight.

By early morning it was already far too hot for sleep and the soda flats glinted and sparkled in the sunlight. Warrior, of course, was still fast asleep, rocking gently to some internal rhythm of his own.

Kush walked around him a few times and then turned to Grandfather. 'I'm not sure if I want to be carried by him after all, at all, at all…'

'Don't worry, the Perceiver and I have worked out a plan to keep Warrior awake. I only hope she can find what she's looking for,' replied Grandfather, pacing up and down in front of us, his paws clasped behind his back. Every now and then he put up his binoculars to gaze up the valley.

Mid-morning was upon us. Warrior was still asleep. Grandfather gazed up the valley again and again and then at last whispered: 'Good, good here she comes.' And across the plain strode our graceful friend. She approached the tree quietly, bent her head down and dropped something in front of Grandfather. We all had a close look to see what it was. It turned out to be a very pungent and mouldy piece of wood; wood that hadn't seen the sun in a long time but had lain deeply buried under wet earth and water-sogged leaves. Winter wood! Yes, it smelled like winter; of frosty nights and damp mornings, of fires that couldn't catch alight...where did the Perceiver find it, when it belonged to Northern cold and Northern forests? Grandfather picked the wood up and waved it in front of the eagle's beak. It woke him instantly.

'Winter! Surely it's not winter yet! I...I can't stay,' he said looking rather confused and beginning to flap his wings sluggishly.

Grandfather laughed richly. 'Well done Perceiver! Where did you find it?'

'I had to dig deep beside a water hole,' she replied smiling rather indulgently at Warrior.

'We've found a way to keep you awake Warrior,' said Grandfather.

'How?' he asked, beginning to perk up considerably.

'The smell of winter!' laughed Grandfather, brandishing the piece of wood. 'Every time you look as if you're about to fall asleep, we'll wave this in front of your beak.'

'Splendid!' cried Warrior loudly, snapping his beak so hard that some chips broke off and fell into the grass. 'Then it's time to depart,' he said and he stretched out his wings and proudly showed us his enormous wingspan. There was enough room on his back for all of us, even Kush.

Grandfather and I turned to bid the Perceiver a sad farewell. 'I am so delighted that Hugill sent us on that tangent...to meet you,' he said.

She fluttered her long eyelashes over her expressive dark eyes, the colour of amber in the sun, and then nuzzled each one of us in turn. 'It has been a supreme pleasure... and filled with such surprises...even for me...'

'I can't take off from the ground with all of you on board,' said Warrior, flying to a branch in line with the giraffe's head. 'Now if your Giraffe friend would lift you up and place you all on my back, then we shall be ready for a lift-off.'

The Perceiver complied and we nestled into the eagle's warm black-brown feathers. At first Warrior wobbled on his thin legs, then he regained his balance and lifted slowly, cumbersomely into the air. We waved back at the Perceiver, who inclined her head a touch. She stayed there watching us, like a tall guardian angel, until she became a brown blob shimmering and dancing on the lake's edge.

CHAPTER THIRTEEN
A STRANGE LAND IN-BETWEEN

Warrior flew high above the lake. Its calm grey surface reflected the surrounding escarpment almost as perfectly as a mirror. It looked so inviting, so cool in the mid-morning sun; only the stretches of soda here and there reminded us of the impossibility of a cooling bathe and of quenching thirsts. Halfway across the lake Warrior's spirits seemed to flag and he slowed down, faltering once or twice. Grandfather quickly leant forward and waved the piece of winter-wood near the eagle's beak. He perked up immediately and picked up speed, lifting higher into the sky.

In spite of the wind rushing past us, the heat was oppressive. It took the edge off our concentration and we became drowsy. I noticed Kush's bright eyes close and then open, and then stay closed. Before I could reach forward to wake him up he suddenly lost his balance and rolled off Warrior's back. Oh no! He was plummeting towards the lake's mirrored surface, confused and unable to get his bearings. Warrior, like some great flying machine, banked and quickly drew in his wings. He turned his head slowly and dived his predatory dive towards Kush. Fortunately Kush's wings had opened slightly and the wind had stretched them out automatically. With a great deal of frantic flapping and squawking he managed to save himself from falling into the lake. Warrior reached him at last and grabbed hold of him with his talons, carrying him high above the lake and only letting go when he thought that the parrot had recovered sufficiently to fly alone.

Kush immediately flew above Warrior and sank down onto the old eagle's back. 'Oh my goodness! Oh my! Oh my! Oh! Oh!' he squawked and shrieked and wailed.

'It's all right,' said Grandfather, patting Kush's livid green feathers, now ruffled and all out of place. But nothing could stop Kush's flow of repeated 'oh my' and 'oh oh'. Grandfather rummaged in a side pocket of his rucksack and pulled out a tiny silver bottle with the words 'FOR DIRE EMERGENCIES ONLY!' written on it. He pulled off the lid and handed the bottle to Kush. 'Just a drop or two on the tip of your tongue Kush, not more, it's very strong.'

Kush immediately obeyed, coughed and spluttered and then smiled broadly. 'Mmmm…how very nice this is. What is it? What is it? Brandy? Elderberry wine?' and was about to gulp the entire contents down, when Grandfather grabbed the bottle from him and stowed it firmly away in the rucksack.

'Never you mind what it is, it's for emergencies only,' and he turned to keep a close watch on Warrior.

We were now approaching the Southernmost tip of the lake. A strange and desolate land lay beyond it: flat and sparsely covered in grey-brown and dirty, dull green scrub. Here and there a lone acacia tree stood out, foliage all matted and threadbare, a meagre offering of protection and shade. It seemed a barren land. It must surely be uninhabited. What animal would choose to live here?

Then, to our infinite surprise, we noticed the feathers. Millions of tiny grey, white and pink feathers were dotted across the plain. They blew this way and that in the hot sultry wind. But there was still no sign of life. In the distance, on either side, we could see the escarpment walls of the Southern Rift. Warrior sighed, his big bird-body sagging suddenly at the thought of yet another lake ahead of us. Grandfather quickly waved the winter-wood near his beak and he perked up a little, though not as much as before.

'Ha,' breathed Warrior suddenly and he froze in mid-air for a few seconds. Ahead of us lay the second of the soda lakes and the end nearest us was stained red.

'We are now in Tanzania!' whispered Grandfather to me.

Warrior flew out over what looked like red liquid and we saw one of the strangest sights I had yet seen on our journey. Thousands and thousands of pink birds with long sinuous necks and perched on thin stalk-like legs walked about, quietly eating away at whatever it was that could possibly have been edible in that sedge and soda clay.

'Turn back! Turn back!' screeched Kush, a green wing stretched over his face, his tiny black eyes peeping through and then shutting in horror. Warrior banked slowly and turned back to the plain, where he landed slowly, falling asleep the instant his wings closed against his exhausted body.

We slipped off his back and onto the ground. In minutes we were surrounded by thousands of birds who had drifted in from the lake, their pink plumage rustling and shivering with curiosity. They formed a silent ring around us, leaving a distance of some six feet in-between. Their eyes were of a luminous yellow with a tiny pin-prick of black in the centre; their bills were heavy and bent inwards, black-pointed; their fat round middles and long sinuous necks were perched on thin pink legs which ended in webbed feet. I tugged Grandfather's tail and whispered: 'My fish-birds! The bird part of the fish!'

'Ah, how very interesting dear Livingstone,' he said.

The strange birds continued to watch us in silence. One or two brave ones would dip their heads down to the ground, to stretch forward for a little sniff before hastily pulling back and lifting high on a stretched neck, eyes turned askance.

Kush was still hiding behind his wing. He leant towards Grandfather and me, whispering out of the corner of his beak: 'Don't like the look of this lot at all, at all, do you?'

'I don't know yet,' replied Grandfather. 'Let's wait and see.'

One of the largest of the birds edged a little closer but darted back as soon as he saw us watching it.

'Look down,' whispered Grandfather.

We did so and after a few minutes, during which we all seemed barely to breathe, the same large bird began a peculiar sideways and backwards approach. We watched his webbed feet come closer and closer and then stop inches away. He must be right over us now. And so he was, because a large bill nosed its way between the four of us. It sniffed the slumbering Warrior first, then the shivering, hiding Kush, then it passed onto Grandfather and me, beginning with our tails and ending at our whisker-tips.

After an unbearable silence the bird spoke at last and in the queerest way, his words rising and falling as his head rose and fell and ending on a high-pitched note: 'ohw era uoy?'

Grandfather and I looked at each other, dumbfounded. What on earth was he saying?

'I beg your pardon?' asked Grandfather politely.

'tahw?' the strange bird said in reply (or so I thought).

What did that mean? Grandfather tried a new tack. He bowed low and pointed a paw at each one of us, introducing us. The bird must have understood a little of what he was trying to do, because he turned and indicated the rest of the flock saying, in rising and dipping tones: 'ew era seognimalf'

'I told you Hugill was nuts…nuts…nuts. This is some kind of joke…he's setting us up,' said Kush angrily, emerging from behind his wing.

The bird looked most offended. He pulled his head back and gave us a sideways look, beginning a slow backwards retreat. Grandfather immediately put up his paw and bowed low again in apology. Somewhat mollified the bird drew nearer. He dropped his head down again, saying: 'era uoy yrgnuh?'

Grandfather shrugged and shook his head incomprehensibly from side to side; the bird followed suit swaying this way and that. All communication went silent for a while.

Suddenly he perked up. 'doof? doof?' He said, opening his bill and closing it again.

'What can he be asking us?' said Grandfather frantically. He rummaged in his rucksack and pulled out a notebook. 'Can you remember all the words he said?'

We told him as many as we could and he wrote them down and examined them.

The bird's head hovered over Grandfather's shoulder, his eyes watching intently. Then he began to sniff the earth, finally sifting up some sand and munching it, saying: 'tae! tae! doof! doof!'

Meanwhile, Warrior had opened his eyes. He watched us all with a look of complete confusion on his face. Then he listened intently as the bird repeated his last sing-song sentence. He examined Grandfather's notebook and then his face brightened and he laughed deeply, his old body shaking. 'ha…ha…ha…ho…ho…ho.'

The bird watched fascinated and then seemed to copy the eagle. 'Ah ah ah oh oh oh'

'Backwards!' I screamed.

'Yes!' said Warrior.

'Well done! Yes, that's it! Look at my notebook,' said Grandfather. 'Flamingoes! Backward-speaking flamingoes! Oh Hugill! What a grand discoverer you are,' he shouted, throwing the notebook in the air and jumping up and down. We all laughed grandly, our ha ha ha's and ho ho ho's mingling wildly with the flamingo's 'ah ah ah's' and 'oh oh oh's

The rest of the flock took up the refrain and the words flounced and bounced from bird to bird, rising and falling as their heads rose and fell, until at last the laughter died away somewhere across the lake.

The flamingo dropped his head again, saying: 'doof?'

'Food,' said Grandfather. 'He wants to know if we're hungry.' He turned to the bird.

'tahw dnik fo doof?' he asked slowly.

The flamingo cogitated deeply over his reply and then said, with a hint of a smile: 'lake food?'

'Now what's he saying?' asked Grandfather, writing the new words down in his notebook. While he did this I noticed a look of puzzlement cross the bird's face.

'You nincompoop!' shrieked Kush. 'He's speaking forward...for you, and you didn't even notice.'

The flamingo bounced up and down looking at us eagerly.

'Oh how silly of me,' laughed Grandfather. 'On! On! On! Ew tonnac tae ekal doof,' and he bowed and produced our ration boxes to show that we still had a supply. The flamingo nodded.

'erehw era uoy gniog?' Asked the flamingo.

'ssorca eht ekal,' replied Grandfather.

'ssorca eht ekal!' shrieked the bird in alarm and he shook his head vigorously, his neck rippling from top to bottom. 'on! on! on! no! no! no!' and he spoke both backwards and forward urgently.

'yhw ton?' asked Warrior sternly, pulling himself together and walking stiffly up to the flamingo.

'flight long!' replied the flamingo forwards.

'woh gnol? asked Warrior, determined to address the flamingo in his own language.

'day and night.'

Warrior staggered backwards at the thought of a night flight. Then he held himself up tall, his wings folded tightly back against his sides and in a voice of great calm and dignity he said: 'We leave at first light. Have you still got the winter-wood Darwin?'

'Er yes…but don't you want to reconsider?' Grandfather asked Warrior cautiously, unwilling to give offence. 'We wouldn't mind by-passing the lake altogether and flying over the escarpment.'

Warrior brushed his words aside. 'You don't understand,' he said shortly. 'This is something Hugill wants me to do. I can see it all now…it's a question of restoring faith. I want your entire chocolate supply at the ready in case of dire need and one or two of your wholemeal biscuits broken into bite-sized pieces.' And with that he fell asleep.

The rest of us had a wonderful evening talking backwards and forwards and upside down and inside out with our delightful new friends. At last, tired but elated we managed to put in a few hours of sleep before the gruelling flight ahead.

CHAPTER FOURTEEN

A VERY GRAND FLIGHT

A hint of yellow fringed the dark blue horizon. It was just before dawn. Our flamingo friend tapped each of us awake with his heavy bill and then bounced his head up and down in a queer sort of bowing movement. 'llew tem, llew tem, eb luferac,' he said sadly.

We all bowed too, in farewell.

'ti sah neeb hcus a taerg erusaelp…lleweraf, lleweraf…' said Grandfather.

He and I climbed onto Warrior's back and he lifted to the topmost branches of an acacia tree, where Kush joined us. There he rested for a few minutes, opening and closing his great wings. Then he gathered all his strength in one gigantic deep breath and with a great Herculean beat of his wings, he rose majestically into the air, lifting high above the plain. Thousands of flamingoes gathered together and waved their pink and white wings wildly. We waved back and as we flew over the red liquid we heard, as if in a dream:

'doG deeps! doG deeps! doG deeps! doG deeps!'

It became fainter and fainter until all that was left was a quaint laughing sound:

'oh oh ah ah oh oh ah ah' and finally the silence of the rushing air and the powerful beating of Warrior's wings.

Grandfather immediately settled down to making two heaps of food at the base of the old eagle's neck: chocolate on the one side and biscuits on the other. The piece of winter-wood, slightly drier now and not as malodorous as before, lay in his one paw.

The red liquid soon gave way to the whites and brown-greys of soda flats and muddy shallows. Warrior exhorted us repeatedly to keep looking ahead at all times. And when we flew over an expanse of flat lake in which clouds and blue sky were mirrored perfectly on its calm surface, he became extremely agitated.

'Don't look down! Watch the sky! Keep an eye on the horizon!' he shouted, his words flying past us like frantic little butterflies searching for a leafy shelter.

Grandfather leant forward and slipped a piece of chocolate into the eagle's beak. 'Don't worry old fellow,' he said, keeping his own voice as level as he could. 'We'll watch the sky and if we notice you mistaking the lake for the sky, we'll let you know.'

'Thank you Darwin…but…but…this kind of lake confuses you, you know.' And he picked up speed a little after the chocolate.

We flew for some hours over that dangerously mirrored surface before it was at last broken up by soda stretches. Warrior faltered only once, dipping his head and preparing to fly down towards the lake. Grandfather waved the winter-wood from one side while I slipped bits of biscuit into the eagle's beak from the other. Warrior quickly pulled up and rose higher into the sky.

'Thought I was going up then,' he said, a shaky chuckle coming up from his craggy old throat.

Towards late afternoon Grandfather insisted that Kush and I have a sleep. 'Tonight will be the real test for us all: no horizon, just a dark lake below and a black sky above; only the stars to guide us and they will be reflected in the lake.'

Kush and I looked at each other in mute terror. We quickly settled further into Warrior's feathers to sleep the afternoon away.

It was dusk when we awoke. The lake had turned a dull gold and the soda and mud stretches were now quite black. After a light snack, I changed places with Grandfather and he took his sleep. Kush and I watched in awe as the great sky turned from a rich coppery red, to dark purple and then to black. Warrior's spirits tangibly lifted as the stars finally appeared, followed reluctantly it seemed by the pale strip of an arched moon.

So absorbed were we in this magnificent stellar display that we were completely unaware that Warrior was gradually sinking towards the starred surface of the lake. It was only when I chanced to look over the side and suddenly saw his huge body reflected in the dark waters below, that I realised that disaster lay ahead of us all.

'Warrior! Warrior!' I screamed, waving the winter-wood in front of his beak.

Kush took up the cry with a squawk and a screech.

Grandfather leapt forward and grabbed the piece of wood from my paws, waving it desperately in front of Warrior. The eagle awakened with a jolt and pulled himself clumsily out of the nosedive. He rose back into the sky, spraying us with his warm tears.

'Don't lose heart now, old friend.' said Grandfather. And he handed Warrior a biscuit and a piece of chocolate from our fast diminishing supply. 'We'll make it.'

'Do you really think so?' sighed Warrior hopelessly.

'Well, Hugill must have thought you could do it and Hugill knows everything!' said Kush, rather sanctimoniously, from the back.

At the mention of the monkey's name, Warrior increased his speed with renewed vigour and determination.

The rest of the long dark night proceeded without mishap. Towards dawn we flew beyond the lake's edge and continued over the land.

'Well done Warrior!' we all shouted, dancing round and round on his back.

'Thank you,' he said, more warm tears flying past us to be absorbed by the dawn sky: a modest indication of his own deep satisfaction. 'Alas…but it's not quite over yet.' He sniffed.

'Why?' asked Grandfather.

'Hugill said I was to fly you over the volcano to the South of the second soda lake and then to bear Eastwards, to the edge of the great Serengeti Plain.'

Grandfather put up his binoculars and gazed ahead. After some miles, he pointed excitedly to the domed top of a volcano. Warrior flew straight over it and we were able to look down into its dark crater.

'Don't linger! Don't linger! I've had enough of volcanic craters!' screamed Kush.

Warrior chuckled and turned away from the volcano, bearing Eastwards. At last we had put the strange land of the lakes behind us. What lay ahead, I wondered.

CHAPTER FIFTEEN

ON THE EDGE OF A PLAIN

Warrior was exhausted. His big body quivered uncontrollably and his wings flapped sluggishly. But his great and glorious achievement in flying us across the two soda lakes spurred him on to complete his mission. He flew us well past the mountainous terrain and then descended slowly towards the edge of the great savannah grassland, which stretched unendingly before us, an ocean of yellows, browns and greens.

He made for a clump of trees and managed to grab hold of one of the topmost branches before falling instantly into the deepest of sleeps; a noisy sleep of loud snores and a high pitched whistle which hissed through the cracks in his beak.

'Well that's that then!' said Kush, flying off Warrior's hot slumbering body and placing himself on an adjacent branch.

Grandfather and I stretched our stiff limbs and gathered our belongings. Just before climbing down, I noticed Grandfather slip the piece of winter-wood into his rucksack. He smiled at me. 'The old bird won't be needing that again. He deserves to sleep for as long as he wishes. And he doesn't need to be reminded of winter ever again either. Besides…I've got used to having it about me…like a talisman you know…' and he shrugged sheepishly.

We climbed across to Kush's cool and leafy perch. Grandfather opened a tin of sardines.

'Ahh this is the life,' sighed Grandfather, stretching himself out across the branch and eating a piece of sardine, sandwiched between two tiny wholemeal biscuits.

'Glad you think so!' said Kush crossly.

'What's the matter Kush?' asked a bemused Grandfather.

'Well, I've had enough of these biscuits of yours for one thing,' he said, taking a reluctant bite. 'And…and I'm missing Hugill. I think he's leading us to the ends of the earth, that's what I think.' And he hopped to the very end of the branch, turning his face away. We heard a tiny sniff.

'Don't cry Kush old friend,' said Grandfather.

'I'm not crying and don't ever tell Hugill that I was,' he said, blinking his eyes rapidly and then brushing them with a green wingtip.

'No…no…we won't say a word about it, but Hugill's not leading us a dance. Wherever he wants us to end up, it's bound to be somewhere rather special, of that you can be quite sure,' said Grandfather.

Kush brightened at this, hopped back to us again and began pecking noisily at a piece of biscuit.

'When you've quite finished,' came a deep and rather bored voice from behind. We whipped round and there, draped elegantly across a low branch of the tree, his tawny fur camouflaged by bark and foliage, was the lion.

'Eek!' shrieked Kush, dropping the biscuit and rushing towards the end of our branch.

'No...no...no,' said the lion, holding up a large paw, 'don't start the chase all over again, I couldn't stand it.'

'What are you going to do to us now that you've got us?' asked Grandfather, shakily grabbing hold of me and holding me firmly to his chest.

'Do?'

'Yes do?'

'Do! What I'm going to do is to give that message I tried to give you in the valley,' said the lion.

'There you are Livingstone and Kush, didn't I say that I thought the lion was not actually chasing us?' said Grandfather triumphantly.

'Well, pity you didn't transmit your thoughts to that daft giraffe,' countered the lion with a haughty lift of his powerful shoulders.

'She's not daft, she's perceptively high, er...I mean highly perceptive. But were you supposed to meet us in the valley?' I asked.

The lion went silent. He shook his head and lay on his back, tickling his huge barrel of a chest. And then he began to laugh; a loud booming laugh which developed into a raucous roar which seemed to lift out of the tree and travel way across the plain. Then he stopped suddenly and rolled into an upright position, his paws dangling over the branch. 'Er no…actually…' he replied.

'Oh.' I said. 'Where were you supposed to meet us?'

'Right here as a matter of fact…' and he threw back his enormous head and laughed again. 'I wanted to travel South with my pride and so I thought I'd look for you, deliver my message and then leave. But that silly giraffe thwarted my plans. I've been lolling around here waiting for you ever since.' And he reached forward and pulled petulantly at an overhanging frond of leaves.

'Well I must say, it's just as well you're only telling us now otherwise we might have missed Warrior and the lakes and the flamingoes,' said Grandfather sternly. 'What is the message anyway?'

'Oh such a silly one really, to have kept me from my family. This is all it is:

Eden is near
But first:
Search for a Weeper in Perpetual Motion.

He's a bit mad your monkey friend, to have expected me to wait around all this time to deliver such nonsense.'

'Is that all?' shrieked Kush, darting backwards and forwards along the branch.

'Wait! wait! I must think about it,' said Grandfather. He thought deeply for a minute and then wrote it down in his notebook. 'Well, at any rate, *Eden is near* must mean that we're reaching the end of the story or is it its beginning? Oh Hugill, what riddles you've woven around us. Is there a Garden of Eden nearby?' Grandfather asked the lion.

The lion yawned and shook the flies off his nose. 'Not as far as I know,' he said, lazily stretching himself out further along the branch.

'Do you have any idea what the last line means?' I asked the lion.

'None whatsoever,' he replied, his head lolling on a paw and his eyes beginning to close.

'Don't you want to be part of this adventure?' I persisted.

'Not really…ahawmmm…' and he yawned again, 'but if you insist.'

'Will you help us find this *Weeper?*'

'If I must I suppose I must…but not now.' And his big body sagged and he was fast asleep.

We were surrounded by snores. Warrior had remained steadfastly asleep throughout the encounter with the lion; his snores and whistles a background chorus to our entire conversation. The lion now joined in with a special snuffling, snorting brand of his own and every time he exhaled, his lips bounced and flapped alarmingly.

'I can't stand this cacophony!' shrieked Kush, 'I'm off…see you later.' And he flew out of the tree and away on an adventure of his own.

‘Looking for berries I have no doubt,’ chuckled Grandfather. ‘Well come on Livingstone, let’s climb down and stretch our legs on the plain.’

Three lionesses snoozed in the shade beneath the trees. They lay on their backs, their paws uppermost and their large heads lolling over to one side. Four boisterous cubs played and fell about around them. We crawled to within a few feet and took it in turns to watch their antics through the binoculars.

Suddenly one of the cubs saw the sunlight reflecting on my magnifying glass. It cocked its head to one side and then bounded over to me, its face filled with curiosity. It stretched out a paw tentatively at first and then dabbed at me, pushing me right over. I burst out laughing and the noise attracted the other cubs. In no time at all I was surrounded by four pairs of shiny black eyes and four wet noses. I disappeared under the grass and slid away from them. They sniffed the grass, heard me move and came after me again. We dashed around the trees and raced some distance away and back again. I was too fast for them and they waddled and fell clumsily over each other in the chase.

We frolicked about happily until the grasses burned gold in the late afternoon sunlight and a light wind rustled across the plain, lapping at grass-tips and tree-tops.

The lion roared mightily and the cubs dashed back to their mothers. The lionesses gazed disinterestedly about them, picked themselves up, stretched and strutted off across the plain with the four cubs bounding along in their wake.

CHAPTER SIXTEEN

A WILDEBEEST'S WEEP (CONTAINING HIS SPEECH)

The lion roared himself awake.

'What was that? What did you say Darwin?' I heard Warrior mumble.

'What was who? Who said what?' asked the lion.

But the only reply was a loud snore and a high pitched whistle. Warrior had fallen asleep again. The lion descended regally to the ground. It was then that we realised just how huge he was. He stood erect, his head up and his mane falling splendidly about him. How that long powerful body belonged on the African plain with its casually upturned tail and a head turned this way and that, mane flicked back.

He waited. We waited. Then he growled softly and called us over with the bare nod of his shaggy head, 'I have an idea of where we could look for this *Weeper.*' So we walked over to him and he inclined his cropped mane towards us, indicating that we should climb up. We grabbed hold of that thick tawny mass of fur and climbed to a spot above his forehead; a forehead that was deeply etched with battle scars.

'I suppose Warrior's all right?' I said, looking up at his slumbering brown form in the tree.

'Yes…yes let him sleep,' replied Grandfather.

Kush came hurtling out of the sky just as we were about to set off and flew past ahead of us, not wanting to join us on the lion's mane.

The lion strutted along the South-Easterly edge of the plain for some miles until we reached a wide river. There he crouched, as if waiting for something. Yet nothing was forthcoming and uncertain as to what we should do, we too sat and waited. It was then that we heard the noise: a thundering vibration which seemed to well up from beneath the earth itself. It came closer and closer until, in the distance, we saw a cloud of dust rising. The thundering increased, the earth shook and out of the cloud emerged thousands upon thousands of blue-grey buck-like beasts. Their sharp little black horns were turned inwards; their shaggy beards hung below long snouts; their pointed hooves leapt and bounded and kicked in their mad dash along the plain towards the river. Without a thought or a backward glance or a hesitation they leapt into the muddy water, their young following, crammed against their mothers' sides. They swam across the river in large solid masses and more kept coming.

'What on earth are those?' asked Grandfather, raising his binoculars.

'They're wildebeest,' said the lion.

'What are they doing?' Grandfather asked the lion in amazement. But the lion just shrugged and shook his head. 'How odd! They don't seem to stop,' Grandfather continued as we watched the great tide of animals pass by. 'They're in continuous motion, Livingstone, that's what they are…that's it!…perpetual motion!'

'Why?' I asked the lion.

'I've never found out,' he said with a bored sigh.

Above the noise of splashing water and grunting we heard a wail: a mournful sound that rose above the rush and drifted towards us, haunting in its sadness.

'*The Weeper in Perpetual Motion*, it must be,' said Grandfather. 'But how are we going to find him in all this crush?'

'I'll fly above them and see what I can see,' said Kush and he hurtled in to the sky, where he rose and fell above the moving mass. Then he flew towards a boulder on the edge of the river and beckoned to us to come. The lion strutted over to him and there in the dust and grime was our *Weeper.* He rested on bent forelegs, his bony haunches in the air. His tail drooped and his grey-blue coat was covered in dust and lay in wrinkles around his neck. His long black snout was tucked in and all we could see were his sharp horns. And all we could hear was a wail, a heartrending wail which tore out of his large chest.

'Boo...hoo...boo...hoo...hoo...' he went, on and on and on. Kush immediately dropped down and pecked at one of his horns.

The wildebeest lifted his head. His large dark eyes were filled to the brim with tears, the fur beneath them quite wet.

'What's the matter?' asked Grandfather.

The wildebeest sighed: 'I'm very old, nearing the end of my lifespan on earth ...and...and...I've never stood still for very long, anywhere. Not, that is, until I met your monkey friend.'

'What?' asked Kush, dropping down next to the wildebeest.

'Yes, isn't it odd, most peculiar! Do you know that this herd has been going round and round this plain and then into the rain forest and back and round and round again for thousands of years?'

'Good grief!' shrieked Kush. 'Can't you stop it?'

'No...we are born and we die in perpetual motion,' and then the wailing' started all over again.

The lion shook us off his head. 'Well, I've done my bit. I can't listen to all this wailing.'

'Thank you for taking us this far...for introducing us to the wildebeest,' said Grandfather, bowing to the lion.

'Ah well, can't say I haven't enjoyed it,' he replied and with a flick of his mane he was off, back across the plain.

We turned to the wildebeest. 'What did Hugill suggest?' I asked.

At the mention of the monkey's name, the wildebeest brightened considerably. 'A holiday…he said I needed a new direction in life and that perhaps you could help me. "Watch out for a parrot and some mice," he said.'

'We can help you! But we need you to help us!' said Kush.

'How can I do that when I know absolutely nothing about anything except how to avoid being trampled on, how to avoid drowning and how to run?'

And he was about to curl his head in again in despair when Grandfather interrupted him: 'Wait…that's it!'

'That's what? What's it?' said Kush.

'Running!' he said, beaming at us. We shook our heads and he continued: 'The wildebeest needs a change and we need someone to run us as fast as possible to Eden.'

'Eden?' asked the wildebeest.

'Yes,' said Grandfather and he told him Hugill's message.

The wildebeest thought for a while. 'Perhaps he means the forest. There is a lovely forest we run past every year. Not many know of it. It's on the edge of the plain. If you're talking about a garden, it's about the best garden I know of in the whole land.'

'Wonderful!' said Grandfather and he grabbed hold of the wildebeest's funny black beard and swung himself onto his head, positioning himself around a horn. Kush and I followed and the wildebeest stopped sniffing and pulled himself up rather grandly. He leapt into the air and almost flew into the river. He swam powerfully across it hardly wetting us at all. Then he pulled himself up the opposite bank and began to run back in the direction we had originally come with Warrior, back towards the escarpment on the edge of the great plain.

'Do you have any idea why your herd runs all the time?' Grandfather asked as we galloped along.

THE WILDEBEEST'S SPEECH

'It's habit and custom. We originally began running to get away from lions and other animals of prey. The more we ran the more efficient we became at running. We've turned it into such a fine art that all else is lost to us. We've forgotten about other things. I want to stop and look at my reflection in the water, but no, I have to drink along the way. I want to sniff each blade of grass I eat, but no, I have to grab at food as I run. I want to smell the wet earthy smell of a newborn wildebeest, but no, even the babies are born running (I don't know to this day how they do it!). It's a collective decision… we have to run as a herd to make the reason why we're running reasonable, if you see what I mean. To stop running is to be unreasonable; to be quite unacceptable to the rest of the group. So we keep at it year after year, season after season until we believe that we cannot possibly survive for one second, even just to smell a flower or watch a butterfly pass by. I want a different sort of life. And is it such a loss if I do stop and enjoy a brief minute watching the swallows fly over or a fish leap out of the river and then get consumed by a lion? Yes, I know it's an odd attitude, quite ridiculous in fact. But you see, the more I run the less I want to run and then the more strange I begin to feel. Hugill said that life was full of the odd ones out. "Take courage and run a different path," he said. But I just went on running and crying and…and… then you found me.'

The wildebeest ended his speech and increased his speed. We reached the edge of the escarpment and the wildebeest ran along it for many miles in a Northerly direction. On and on he ran, through the dusk light and into the night, not stopping for a rest or to take a breath. He ran with an urgency and a vigour and, with mounting excitement, he said at last, 'The forest is not far.'

'Oh good. Perhaps we can have a rest on the edge of it. Sleep until dawn. Much lies ahead of us,' said Grandfather.

'Do we have to?' asked the wildebeest.

'Yes, you must stop!'

'Yes, I know…I mean that's what Hugill suggested… But, do you think I ought? It's all making me rather nervous. I've been moving for so long perhaps I won't know how to come to a proper, complete stop,' he wailed.

'Don't worry, leave it to us.'

After a few more miles we reached the edge of the forest. 'Look there! There's a nice patch of grass…take us over there!' I said.

The wildebeest raced towards the glade. But he was going much too fast.

'Stop! Stop!' shouted Grandfather.

'I can't!' the wildebeest shouted in a panic.

So Grandfather and I pulled hard at the fur on his head, while Kush frantically tugged at his horns with his wings. At last the wildebeest began to slow down. Then he skidded and came to such a sudden stop that we all flew over his head and landed in the soft sweet-smelling grass.

'Well done!' we shouted.

The wildebeest merely beamed at us and then he buried his long snout in the lush grass.

'Now that wasn't too difficult, was it?' asked Grandfather, patting the tip of the wildebeest's one horn.

The wildebeest winked but not for a second did he extract his nose from the grass. We stretched out and fell into a deep sleep.

CHAPTER SEVENTEEN

EDEN GAINED

I heard a rustle behind me. I sat up and looked round. It was the wildebeest. He was still sniffing the grass profoundly and then munching a few blades at a time, savouring each varied taste. Had he rested at all I wondered? I looked into the forest. Its cool, dark green depths were thick with bird sounds mingled with animal grunts and shrieks and howls. Here and there I could see a shaft of early morning sunlight penetrating the heavy foliage, picking out the rich and variant forest greens: topical jade, olive, iridescent lemon; and it touched lightly the dark creeper, the black-brown bark and the whispy fungus.

Grandfather woke up and stretched from top to tail. 'Where's Kush?' he asked.

I looked around but Kush was nowhere to be seen. I asked the wildebeest whether he had seen him, but he hadn't. 'Perhaps he's looking for berries in the forest. It looks like the kind of forest to have berries and other fruits,' I said.

'Mmmm…well, we'll just have to start without him. He's bound to catch up with us,' replied Grandfather.

We climbed back onto the wildebeest's head and entered the great forest. A little way in we crossed a stream and Grandfather insisted on a swim and then we refilled our water-bottles with fresh water before continuing our journey. The wildebeest picked his way through dense undergrowth, worked his way in and out of filigreed creeper and crossed many streams and rivulets.

I was right about the fruit. We were surrounded by giant fig, papaya and banana trees, and the fruit hung tantalisingly above us. We could see monkeys swinging joyously from branch to branch, grabbing fruit as they went along. Was Hugill with them I wondered? Around us everything teemed with animal life: a large forest hog suddenly swayed across our path, his thick blubbery flesh wobbling as he moved; a small family of impalas were drinking from a stream; nearby a rhino nibbled at some grass; a baboon troupe bounced past us and away into the trees; a crashing of bushes and a cracking of twigs and we could just make out three young elephants marching massively through the forest, now trumpeting, now pulling at thick juicy leaves. We passed a clump of trees filled with weaver's nests. And the forest was dense with birdsong and animal noise. This was Hugill's "Eden". It had to be.

We made for a large tree in a small glade. While the wildebeest buried his snout in the long, luscious grass we slipped off his back and leant against its ample trunk. It was then that we heard an extraordinary conversation. It began with a loud cackle and then a 'hss…hss…hss…hss.' The one voice said: 'Shshtelecommunicationsh.'

And then another voice said, 'Hss...hss…hss…why that's stupendousss, what does it mean?

'No idea…but it'sh the longesht word I know,' came the other voice.

We looked around. I was sure one of the voices belonged to Kush. Then came a sudden shriek, followed by a burp, followed by an 'oops!' and a green form fell out of a small tree nearby, landing at our feet. It was Kush! He lay with his wings stretched out and his beak wide open; his eyes were shut tight and his head lolled from side to side.

'Oh dear,' came the other voice, still in the tree. 'He had one too many…hss… hss…hss…hsssss.' We looked up and gazing down at us, smiling sweetly, was a long green snake. 'The fruit, you know…from the sacred Marula tree, you know. They're quite potent. I did try to stop him from eating too many,' she said apologetically.

'Oh you can't stop Kush once he gets going…berries and fruits are his passion,' I said.

The snake looked at me and hissed delightedly over the word 'passshshion'.

'Ooo what a lovely word. Do you like words? I love them…with a passshshion…hss…hss…hss. Particularly long words. "Anthromorphic" is one of my special favourites, and of course, "anthropocentric". And she hissed and stuttered over the 'centric' part of the word. 'Then there are some good standbys: 'backward looking... barbarous...barbarity...barbarism...don't the b's sound just deliciousss?'

'Yes,' I said. 'What about: 'circumlocution... circumference...circumnavigation?'

Her forked tongue leaped out at me in sheer delight and she curled it over and around my three long words. 'My unending challenge is to find a word as long as my body and do you think I can? It's impossible. I'll have to try Russian one day, perhaps they have extraordinarily long words. Do you think they do? Would they roll easily off the tongue I wonder?'

'I don't know,' I replied. Then I had a bright idea. 'I know! You could speak very quickly, leaving out all the punctuation marks. Like this:

Imlookingforanextraspecialunbelievablyinfinitelylongword,'

'Oh that's a wonderfulmagnificentlyintelligentidea,' said the snake, copying me. 'Shall I put some choice ones together and you can see if it's as long as my body?' She asked.

'Yes, let's go!'

The snake began:

'Inthebestofallpossibleworldslivethebestofallpossibleanimals notquitebarbarouscertainlynotanthropocentricsplendiforously spontaneousalwayswiseandjollyeccentricwithoutbeingobtuse antrhopomorphicatanytimedayornightnevercensoriousorcritical characteristicallyuninhibitedandperpetuallyfree...hssss.'

And she hissed and gasped for breath: 'Now, how was that?'

'I think you've done it,' I replied.

Meanwhile Kush lay in the grass watching us. He stood up and wobbled alarmingly.

'What? What? What wash thatsh you shaid? Shay it again,' he said, slurring and slurping over his words.

Grandfather and I lay back in the grass and laughed uncontrollably.

The snake twisted herself into a knot with sheer joy at discovering a way to string together the longest word in the world and then she said to him: 'I couldn't repeat that my dear Kush...I'll have to think up another one. Let me see,' and she thought for a while, 'what about this one?

Tobeginatthebeginningofastoryisafearfulborebe-causetheendalwayshastobefoundbuttoturnitupside-downandinsideoutandtolookforabeginningistoneverre-alllycometotheendatallitsacircumlocutorywayofcircum-ambulatingawayfromcompletionandoffindingaperfect-methodofkeepingtheheartofatalealive.'

Grandfather clapped his paws in delight: "Do you know, what you've just said reminds me of a spider we met in a valley?'

'Oh, how odd,' said the snake, hanging limply after her last grand effort.

'I like the bit about circum...circum...now what was that you said?' he asked.

'Quite obvioushly it was shircumambushlating,' said Kush and he looked at Grandfather as if he were indeed quite stupid.

'Oh Kush,' I laughed. 'That fruit has made you tipsy. You'll have to sleep it off.'

'Shleep! Shleep! Me shleep when we've shtill got to find Hugill,' and he burped and keeled over onto his back, his beak wide open and his stiff little tongue sticking out straight in front.

'We'll just have to wait until he recovers. How about throwing some of that fruit down to us?' Grandfather asked the snake.

'Are you absolutely sure?' she said.

'Yes. We'd love to try a little.'

The snake slithered higher up the tree, wrapped her tail-end round one of the branches and gave it a shake. A large pile fell about us. And then she disappeared, returning with a bunch of bananas in her mouth. This she threw down to us too. 'Would you like a papaya?' And off she went again without waiting for a reply, only to return with the glossy yellow fruit in her mouth.

The fruit piled up in front of us and we had a prodigious midday feast. A full tummy and the soporific effects of the Marula fruit soon weighed heavily on us and it was not long before Grandfather was snoring loudly. The wildebeest had slunk away behind the tree trunk, to grunt profoundly. I lay back and gazed up at the tiny mosaic of blue sky which peeped here and there through the luxuriant foliage above, at the snake curled languidly, happily around her branch; at the heap of fruit lying about me and then I wondered dreamily whether I could ever possibly leave this forest, Hugill's "Eden".

'That's it!' shouted Grandfather, waking suddenly and scattering papaya pips and banana peels.

'What's it?' I asked in alarm.

'It's slowly beginning to hang together,' he replied.

'What is?'

'Hugill's messages: the spider's never-ending web, the meaning of the snake's second (circular) sentence and Eden.'

'Eden?'

'Yes! If you turn the letters round you get Ende... the beginning and the end are one. I think that's what he meant by his first message. Now what was it again?' And he searched in his rucksack for that first message given to us by Kush so long ago. Out it came at last, all crumpled and stained. 'Yes this is the bit:

Beginnings are never where or what they seem
and they might never end

The beginning hasn't just been at the beginning, where you might expect it to be. It's been there with us all along and it seems to join up with the ending. But why? Why? The snake said that it was a way of keeping the heart of a tale alive. But why?' And he lay back in the lush grass whispering 'Why?' over and over to himself until the words tumbled over each other to become mingled with his snores and to disappear somewhere at the back of his throat. I too lay back and pondered Grandfather's words. Why did Hugill want us to think that beginnings and endings can become indistinguishable? Oh dear, it was all so difficult. I stretched out in the long grass and soon everything became distinctly green, even my thoughts and it no longer seemed to matter.

CHAPTER EIGHTEEN

NUTS...NUTS...AND MORE NUTS

'Wake up! Wake up!' It was Kush and he was slapping my face with his wingtip.

I groaned and rolled away.

'It's time to move on, it'll soon be dusk and we still have to find Hugill!' and he pulled my tail fiercely with his beak, trying to get me to stand up.

'It's no use Kush. I've had too much fruit and I can't move,' I wailed, pulling my bruised tail back.

Kush then tried Grandfather, but he didn't even respond and continued to snore loudly. Kush paced up and down in front of us, his wings hanging limply at his side. Then he sniffed dejectedly at our pile of fruit.

'Have you gone off fruit Kush?' I asked with a giggle.

'No...not quite...just some,' and he flew into a branch. 'Ah well,' he sighed, ruffling his feathers. 'I suppose I'll just have to sleep.' And he shut his eyes and buried his head under one wing. It wasn't long before I too drifted off, on a tide of bananas and papayas in a boat made of words lying at odd angles: upside-down, vertical and back-to-front.

It was while I was trying to decipher the words on this boat that I felt a sharp sting on my left thigh. 'Ouch!' I screamed out. Then I felt another one on my head. 'Ouch! Stop it Kush!'

'I'm not doing anything!' he shrieked back.

Well something was definitely being hurled at me and more of whatever it was kept coming. By now Grandfather and I were both hopping up and down trying to get away.

Kush, who was also being rained upon, had covered himself protectively with both wings.

'They're nuts! Nuts! I mean, they're real nuts!' Kush shouted. And they were: big fat glossy nuts. Hundreds now lay about us.

At last the hail of nuts stopped and we were able to look up into the trees to see who the perpetrators of this deed were. Ranged about us in the branches above were about thirty brown monkeys with black faces. They were laughing at us, bearing sharp little white teeth.

'Hugill's cousins,' whispered Grandfather.

One by one they swung down to the ground, where they sat on their haunches in a large circle, watching us intently. The largest of the troupe, whom we supposed was the leader, detached himself and hopped over to us. He picked up a nut and cracked it expertly between his teeth and then handed it to Grandfather. He did the same for Kush and me. Even the wildebeest, whose determined snout could be seen peeping from behind the trunk, was treated to one. The snake merely watched the proceedings with a look of intense amusement on her face.

'Do they speak?' Grandfather asked her.

'Oh yes. Once they get going they never stop. An irrepressible bunch they are. But they like to take a long look at everything first,' replied the snake, resting her throat on the branch.

'Ah...but you're quite wrong snake,' said our nut-giving monkey shrilly. 'This is after all rather a short look...it's only about two feet short. One of the shortest I'd say. We gave them a long look from high up in the trees.' And he put a well-shaped black hand to his mouth, snickered behind it, his shoulders shaking.

'Confound it! Stop confusing me!' said the snake.

'Oh Snake! Dear Snake! We don't want to confound or confuse just beguile and amuse in the idle time before the moon comes out,' said the monkey, reaching up a long arm to stroke her gently.

'How can time be idle?' I asked mischievously.

'Oh well done, now you're playing the game,' said another monkey, hopping forward eagerly.

'Well it's quite obvious,' replied Grandfather. 'It's what you do with the time on your paws that counts,' and he frowned at me.

But I couldn't stop. 'Oh Grandfather,' I laughed. 'You can't 'do' anything with time and you can't hold it in your paws.'

The monkeys shrieked with laughter all around us.

'No you're not, you're speaking in semaphore, if you want to hold time in your paws that is,' laughed another monkey. 'Is it heavy?' she then asked.

'Is what heavy?' asked Grandfather.

'That bit of time in your paws. The bit you say you're holding,' and the monkey pointed at Grandfather's paws.

We all looked at them.

'It all depends…,' he said obscurely, rubbing his paws together hastily, as if 'time' had indeed come alive and he wanted to rub it away and hoping at the same time that they would change this peculiar subject. Luckily they did.

Another monkey hopped forward suddenly: 'What's infinite, can double back on itself, knot and go round and round?'

We all thought deeply for a few minutes.

'I give up!' I said at length.

'An unending tail,' and all the monkeys laughed, first showing white teeth and then covering them, so as not to offend.

'A tail or a tale?' I asked.

'Oh either will do,' he replied.

Kush had remained determinedly silent throughout the interchange. Then he puffed up his feathers and pushed his way forward. 'Have you any idea where Hugill Macauley is?' he asked haughtily.

The first monkey replied: 'I had the idea, but I haven't got it anymore.'

'What haven't you got anymore of?' asked Kush, backing away from what was clearly going to be yet another bit of confusing word-play.

'The idea.'

'What idea? I never said anything about an idea at all! At all! at all!' and Kush began to ruffle his feathers.

'Yes you did,' chuckled the monkey.

'I did not!'

'Yes, you distinctly asked me whether I had an idea about Hugill's whereabouts and I'm trying to tell you I don't have an idea. I did have an idea about Hugill's whereabouts but it's gone,' continued the monkey.

'Where's it gone?' asked Kush, now obstinately trying to gain the upper hand in the argument, even if it cost him his wingtips.

'The idea of Hugill and his whereabouts left when Hugill left.'

'When Hugill's whereabouts left where?' continued Kush.

'Well, if I knew where Hugill's whereabouts went to, then I would still have an idea about Hugill whereabouts, wouldn't I?' said the monkey, reaching out to give Kush a tiny pat.

'Now you see what I mean,' said the snake, lazily unwinding a knot at the end of her long body:

'Irrepressbleargumentativetautologicalobfuscatory-confusingtothepointofdistractionanalyticalbeyondfrus-tration…hsss.'

And she slithered away into the trees.

We turned back to the monkeys to try our luck with them again. They all hopped closer, eager for more conversation…if that's what it was.

'If you haven't any ideas about Hugill's whereabouts,' asked Grandfather, choosing his words very carefully, 'then have you any ideas about Hugill at all, at all?' and he sounded distinctly like Kush on the very edge of a panic.

'Ahh, now that's different. We do still have some ideas left about Hugill, haven't we?' said the monkey leader turning to the rest, all of whom nodded and hopped about on their haunches. 'That is, he left some behind.'

'What ideas did he leave behind?' Grandfather asked cautiously.

'You'll have to come with us to find them.'

'Anything! Anything!' said Kush, waving his wings desperately at the monkeys.

'Oh I thought we were looking for ideas, not things. But now that you mention it, something does come into it: a very special large thing. But that will come later…'

'Could you show us these ideas and things?' Grandfather asked.

Without even replying, the monkey grabbed Grandfather and me and placed us on his shoulders. We said goodbye to the wildebeest, who had remained in more or less hiding throughout, and disappeared into the branches of the Marula tree. Kush and the entire troupe followed close behind.

As we moved gracefully through the trees, higher and higher, I noticed that this night in the forest was cold. It was so cold that it had a sharp biting edge to it.

'I don't see any sharp biting edges,' said the monkey as he leapt from branch to branch. I shivered and held on tight. Did I speak aloud? No, I'm sure I did not. How odd. There was something strange about Hugill's cousins; very strange. I had the distinct feeling that they weren't just playful and silly.

The monkey took us deep into the forest and then, selecting one particularly tall tree, he climbed right to the very top, to where the foliage thinned out. 'Ahh' breathed Grandfather as we broke through, almost reaching the sky itself. We were able to look across to the edge of the forest. Beyond it lay the African plain, now a ghostly grey in the light given off by the stars and a slowly bulging moon.

'I suggest you three take a small nap,' said the monkey placing Grandfather and me on a branch next to Kush.

'Where to?' I asked, giggling.

'Well,' laughed the monkey in return, 'turn your mind's eye inwards and look for the point furthest away from you…that's where to take it.'

'But…but…I've had enough sleep,' said Kush. 'I've slept all afternoon. Besides, you said you were going to take us find those idea things you mentioned.' And he wailed with frustration.

The monkey softly patted Kush's ruffled feathers and then he tickled him just below his beak and slightly to the side. Kush immediately calmed down and turned his head away so as to get the full benefit of the tickle. His eyes closed and then opened a little and then stayed closed. Grandfather and I looked at the monkey in amazement. He merely smiled at us. 'Now don't forget, look for the point furthest away from you,' he whispered and then disappeared into the trees to join his friends on a night of foraging for more nuts, I supposed.

CHAPTER NINETEEN

TO THE FURTHEST POINT AND BACK

I tried. I tried very hard to do as the monkey had instructed. But each time I looked inwards, for the furthest point away from myself, I came back to the hard branch, the stars and the pale moon; to the cold air and the chatter of animals below. I looked at Grandfather, he was breathing deeply, his mouth slightly open. He had obviously succeeded. Oh dear, perhaps I had better try again. I settled myself more comfortably on the branch and nestled closer to Grandfather for warmth. This time I seemed to travel quite a long way in the grey shadows between dream and wakefulness. Just when I thought I had nearly reached that far-off point, I came up against something sharp. I sat bolt upright. Everything at first seemed just as I had left it. But was it?

While I felt I was on the branch, I also felt that I wasn't quite there at all. I looked around very carefully. In fact, I was no longer on the branch, I was sitting on a blue-grey desert and our tree had quite disappeared.

The sand lay flat and still and where sky and land caressed all was muted green. There was a faint rustle of leaves in the air; a mere vestige of the forest that had been. This must be it, I thought. I have reached the furthest point at last.

'Did you also feel something sharp?' came a rather hollow voice from behind me. I jumped up in fright.

'Oh Grandfather are you here as well?'

'Of course I'm here. Where else should I be?'

'I…I don't know…'

Then Kush suddenly hopped over to us. 'Did you two poke me with something sharp or did I dream it?' he asked, blinking his eyes rapidly.

'I don't think it was a dream because we all felt it,' I replied ,'unless, of course, we dreamt each others' dreams.'

'Now Livingstone! Come down to earth. Let's not drift off into fantasy,' said Grandfather phlegmatically.

'Well, it's extremely hard not to,' I replied, pointing at the warm bluish-grey sand beneath us.

It was only then that Grandfather and Kush realised that we were no longer where we had been. Kush quickly buried his face under his wing. Grandfather sank to his knees in amazement. He dug his paws into the sand and lifted some to his nose, breathing deeply.

'Strange…this sand smells a bit like those lotus-flowers,' he said.

I too smelled the sand. Yes, he was right and in an instant I remembered my dream on the lake. 'You don't think we are actually dreaming?' I asked hesitantly, not really wanting an answer.

'Certainly not! We're all in this together so we couldn't possibly be,' replied Grandfather, making a determined effort to maintain calm.

'Oh good, now I can enjoy it,' I replied.

'Well, I don't like it at all,' wailed Kush, his head still tucked under his wing.

Grandfather gazed at the desert through his binoculars and then passed them on to me. The pallid sky above us was emptied of moon and stars. And apart from some black humps on the horizon, the desert landscape was desolate. We decided to inspect the humps. The sand was soft underfoot as we drifted in their direction. Here and there it twinkled blue, green and silver in the unearthly light. The air, redolent of lotus flowers, was fresh but not cold, comfortably warm without being too hot.

As we drew near we saw that the black humps were the members of monkey troupe. When we reached them they hopped around us, chattering and laughing excitedly. Then the monkey leader commanded them to silence and they obeyed without a murmur.

'Where are we?' I asked.

'Why, you are where I told you to go,' replied the monkey.

'Did Hugill want us to come here?' asked Kush.

'Yes…he wanted us to introduce you to a few ideas.'

'Are we in the land of ideas?' I asked.

‘Yes, something like that,’ smiled the monkey.

‘Good grief!’ shouted Kush. ‘Am I not speaking at all then, at all, at all?’

The monkey smiled again: ‘Not really. We’re all just swapping ideas. It’s something we monkeys are able to do. All animals do it but they don’t know they’re doing it. We do. We have the special privilege of knowing we’re doing it all the time. We can move from playing with language, as we did in the forest, to playing with ideas and back again.’

‘Are we really here as ourselves?’ I asked, pulling at my tail and then examining my little mouse-body.

‘You are here in the form you imagine yourself to be,’ replied the monkey.

‘It’s all very blue and grey up here, or rather in here.’ I said, looking around.

‘Yes, quite a calm place to be. But come, I want to show you something.’

The monkey led us to another part of the desert and we saw the old wildebeest leaning against the tree trunk. He was fast asleep and snoring loudly.

‘I didn’t know he was here too,’ said Grandfather, surprised.

‘He’s not, you’ve just thought of him,’ replied the monkey.

‘Oh did I?’

‘Now listen carefully,’ continued the monkey.

We listened. First we heard a buzzing noise. And then a rather gruff voice saying: ’Grandfather? Livingstone?

Kush? Where are you? Are you all right?' It was the wildebeest calling to us.

'We're here, in the desert! Come and join us!' I shouted.

The wildebeest yawned, 'Oh good. I'm so glad they're safe...' and the buzzing noise came back and he disappeared. The monkey smiled serenely.

'Can't he come to us?' asked Grandfather.

'Oh no! We've helped you to find him. He can't come and look for you, he has no idea where you are.' The monkey then led us further across the desert, to a large acacia tree. On a low branch was the lion and at the top was Warrior. They were both apparently deeply asleep.

'I wonder where Darwin, Livingstone and Kush are?' said Warrior, half to himself.

'When I last saw them they were comforting that silly old wildebeest,' yawned the lion, also speaking more to himself than to the eagle, almost as if he were answering his own question.

'I wonder if they've reached their destination?' said Warrior again.

I decided to intervene. 'No we haven't yet! We're in a desert and...and in the Garden of Eden...' I shouted.

Of course, they couldn't reply, but then Warrior wobbled slightly on his branch, 'Mmm...could have sworn I heard something,' he said.

'Did I hear someone call?' asked the lion.

'I think I'm going to find them and see what happens on this adventure,' said the eagle.

He awakened and lifted rather clumsily into the air and flew towards us. The lion slumbered on.

'So, you see how it works?' asked the monkey. 'They didn't know they were communicating with each other, but they were and it has indirectly helped Warrior back into your adventure.'

And then the monkey began to dance in a circle round us. He leapt and frolicked round and round. As he did so he lifted his hands lightly into the air and seemed to pull pictures from nowhere. We saw the leopard sitting on a rocky outcrop; the ostrich and the zebra walking across a great brown plain; the bat hanging upside down from a branch; the dear Perceiver gazing into the distance...as if in a magic circle, he recalled to us all the scenes of our adventure; one after another each precious moment was revealed to us... round and round and round...

Then the monkey suddenly stopped, he turned to me and gazed deeply into my eyes. 'Ask me your question, Livingstone, don't hesitate.'

How did he know? I looked on him in awe and then dared to ask: 'Well...what I wanted to know was who gave you monkeys this special knowledge or insight and why have only you got it?'

'Ahhh...it was a gift...,' and the monkey's voice trailed away mysteriously. He did not seem to want to say more.

'But how lucky you all are! It's obviously a special gift. For a favoured species, perhaps?' Grandfather asked politely. The monkey didn't reply, so Grandfather continued: 'It is strange that *Humans* haven't got this ability. Don't you think it's rather odd Livingstone? Kush? It seems that *Humans* have missed out somehow.'

The monkey just giggled quietly as though he knew something we didn't.

'It's so kind of you to take us on such an unusual journey,' said Grandfather. 'We will treasure the experience always.' As he finished speaking he suddenly began to behave in a most peculiar way. I watched, fascinated. First he hopped about and then he rummaged in his pocket, pulling out a nut. This he tried to crack between his teeth. He kept at it for quite some time in a trance; struggling with the oversized nut to do the impossible, for a mouse anyway.

At last the monkey shook him slightly and took the nut away. 'I'm afraid you won't be able to do that,' he said.

Grandfather shivered from top to tail. 'Oh...oh dear...for a minute I thought I was turning into a monkey. If I stay here any longer I think that's what will happen!'

The monkey then turned to Kush and began stroking his ruffled feathers gently. 'Kush, dear Kush, something is bothering you too, do tell us.'

'If it's so easy to think up our friends for us and then find them, why can't we find Hugill this way?'

'Ahh...what a devoted friend you are and how lucky Hugill is to have you. He will call us when he is quite ready.'

Then he gathered us about him. 'It's time to go back to the forest. There is still the second stage to this little journey. Shut your eyes and follow me.'

I felt a sharp pain in my head and woke up to find myself lying very close to Grandfather, encircled by his one arm. Both he and Kush were asleep. It was still night. The stars were back. But why should they have left? And there was the moon! But why should I have thought it wouldn't be there? We were on the branch too; its hard rather damp surface confirmed that fact. And the forest; the great beautiful forest rustled and whispered about us just as before.

Grandfather stirred at last. He sat up and looked about him, up at the stars and the moon, at the branch we were on and then at the forest. He frowned and looked at me intently and then away. There was an uneasy silence between us.

Kush suddenly wobbled dangerously on the branch. He slipped and lifted up into the air, flapping his wings frantically. Then he descended and examined the branch closely, pecking suspiciously at the bark. 'I thought I was in a blue desert. How odd! Must have been dreaming!' he said.

'Well if that's where you thought you were then I must have been in your dream, because I was in the same blue desert,' I said.

'And so was I,' said Grandfather with a worried frown.

'Perhaps we all dreamed each other's dream…do you know, I said that before? I said that to both of you in the desert,' and I grabbed Grandfather by the tail. 'Grandfather! Did we or didn't we dream it all up?'

'I don't know Livingstone, I just don't know,' he replied.

A disembodied laugh came from the surrounding trees. We peered deeply into the foliage and after a while managed to make out some black shadows. One of the shadows leapt out at us. It was the monkey leader! He sat down on our branch and reached over to give Kush's neck a little tickle. Kush immediately looked at him, his red-rimmed eyes blinking in alarm. He ruffled his feathers and hopped backwards a few paces. The monkey grinned at him, and then turned to us, saying politely, 'I wonder whether Warrior and the lion will make it to the forest?' Grandfather and I looked at each other. It couldn't have been a dream then, since the monkey was there too. We must have reached the furthest point after all.

'Have we been on this branch for a long time? Is…is it still the same night?' I asked the monkey.

The monkey patted the top of my head softly with one black finger. 'You've only been on this branch for a few minutes,' he replied.

I looked at him searchingly. Our visit to the desert must have happened in the twinkling of an eye, I thought.

The monkey nodded and then winked at me and for one second, as I gazed deeply into his black white-rimmed eyes, a vast blue-grey desert opened up before me. Breathless, I felt myself fall towards it. The monkey picked me up and held me firmly in his hand. The desert slowly receded and the forest noises reasserted themselves. 'Come,' he said, placing Grandfather and I on his shoulders, 'it's time to find a large friend who waits patiently beside a river.'

CHAPTER TWENTY

THE WEIGHT OF AGES

Our nocturnal journey through the densely dark forest began. Kush hovered above the monkey as he leapt agilely from tree to tree, seizing hold of the branches expertly and surely with his shapely hands, or gripping with curled toes and tail. Once he pretended to grab at the snake instead of the branch above. 'Impertinent primate!' she hissed at him before slithering away into the secretive blackness around us. The monkey chuckled delightedly to himself, his laughter picked by the other members of the troupe so that their giggles rose and fell as they leapt and bounded along.

We descended to the lower branches of the trees where, at last, we came upon the river: oily-black and still. We followed its meandering course until we came into an area bathed in a shaft of moonlight. Here the moon had found an unbroken passage through the foliage to touch leaf-tips and water surfaces with muted silver tones.

At the centre of the light and at the river's edge stood a large elephant quietly hosing down her huge dark form with water drawn up in her trunk. And as she lifted and lowered her head, powerful tusks proudly pointed seemed to slice at the light, to cut the air in two.

'There she is!' whispered the monkey, stopping in the fork of a tree to look on in awe at her massiveness. He climbed slowly towards her and then hung down, just above her head.

'Oh One Who Waits In Patience Beside The River, we have come.'

The elephant turned her head towards him and gazed at us from large eyes of an unfathomable depth which sagged and fell away into a myriad of wrinkles. She nodded and curled her trunk upwards. The monkey slipped into its crook and beckoned Kush to do the same. Her tusks gleamed white on either side of us and strange gurgling noises travelled up and down her trunk.

She continued to watch us in silence and the minutes were swallowed up in the immutability of that gaze; it was as if time itself had become absorbed into her massiveness, pulling her further into the earth. And when at last she spoke, her words broke from her in large round whispers. 'Ahh...so your quest is nearing its end...' she said.

Even Kush refrained from intruding upon the silence which followed.

The monkey leant forward and began stroking her trunk lightly; caressing her skin as if it were indeed velvet to the touch rather than dry and leathery. At the same time he looked into her eyes, drawing nourishment and energy from whatever he found in those ancient pools, warm brown and measureless. And as I too looked into them, I believed I could see a great volcano erupt, pouring molten lava over the earth; and gigantic mountains push upwards, forming valleys and cliff walls, where all had been flat before; and vast ancient plains stretching into the distance, with dinosaurs and strange earthbound birds, flying fishes and creeping creatures ambling and gambolling along from end to end.

But that was not all, I saw something else: a monkey with an organ, waving at an elephant. Hugill and Fayum! Could it be? And then I saw an eagle sweeping out of a grey sky. I reached forward wanting to see more and more; how first life forms began and the transformations from one life into the next, and the next, and the next… I felt as if I was falling, falling into those dark pools of memory. Grandfather quickly grabbed my tail and the monkey put a protective hand up.

The elephant swayed a little, lifting one lumpen foot, then another, to lighten her great load. And as if she knew what we had just seen, she spoke again, in liquid tones, the words seeming to come from the bottom of the river: 'I remember everything, absolutely everything…it's such a burden you know.' Her body sagged even further towards the earth and she blew whirlpools in the water. 'All stories are borne in my memory, without beginning and without end; the spirit of each life remains forever embedded in my remembrances.' And as she whispered these words to us, it was as if the trees too had overheard, because they suddenly started rustling and shivering where there was no wind. And a ripple moved across the river, to lap gently at her feet.

Entranced, Grandfather said to the elephant, 'Therefore, there is no end to any life or to any story while they are forever remembered. The beginnings become absorbed in the endings, which become absorbed in the beginnings. Just as the snake has said and as the spider's web showed. Oh Hugill, what greatness you have found! Do you see Livingstone? Kush? Do you see what Hugill has found? While the spirit of each life is remembered, it is carried from generation to generation without end. Each new life carries with it the spirit of older lives, lives going right back in time. It's a great pattern of continuity. And that's why the beginnings of life stories are not where or what they seem and they might never end.' And he sighed, sinking back into the monkey's neck. Then he continued: 'A vast repository, Livingstone and Kush, we have before us a repository of time, of events and of continuity itself. Oh wonder of wonders.'

And then it was that I understood why, to chance to look into those eyes, was to see far down the centuries.

'Shsh…listen,' said the monkey.

At first we heard nothing and then the haunting notes of an organ drifted towards us through the forest gloom and black night. The trees seemed to lift soundlessly in response and even the river kept up its rippling and lapping.

Kush immediately started flapping his wings. 'It's Hugill! Oh and he's so close! Just beyond the trees! Come! Come!' he squawked urgently.

I looked into the elephant's eyes but they had misted over and were now half hidden by heavy lids. She sighed lightly, joyously and swung her trunk to the music.

CHAPTER TWENTY- ONE

THE CALL

'It is the call,' said the monkey, looking in the direction of the sound. He carried us quickly to the elephant's neck and helped Kush onto her brow as she began to move towards the sound, rocking rhythmically from side to side through the darkened forest. We rounded a large clump of thick bush and there, staring at us all and expectantly waiting in the gloom, was the dear, dear Perceiver. Her long neck quivered in delight when we at last drew level with her.

'Oh Perceiver! Dear Perceiver, you here too? What adventures we have had,' said Grandfather.

She inclined her head. 'So I've heard tell…so I've heard…,' and she fell in beside the elephant.

The trees began to thin out. We had reached the edge of the forest. The sky had lightened, the dark night-blue gradually paling above the savannah grassland. Dawn was not far off. And still the music drew us along, from low hillock to open plain; round rocky outcrop and through dense bush. Yet of distance there was none, or so it seemed, only the music and the movement.

'Have I made it? Oh dear! Have I made it?' came an urgent cry from above and Warrior hovered over us looking for a place to settle. The monkey beckoned to him and he landed on the elephant's ample behind. Grandfather and I waved and he snapped his beak excitedly in a noisy wordless reply.

We crossed the plain towards the music and soon found ourselves on the very edge of a gorge. We gazed intently into its darksome depths; depths which harboured the very source of the music.

'That must be the *Olduvai Gorge*, Livingstone!' whispered Grandfather, pointing excitedly into the gorge. 'We've reached the *Olduvai Gorge*! What can Hugill have found down there? That's where *Human* origins lie. Did you know that *Humans* began in Africa, Livingstone? Perhaps right in that very gorge. Millions of years ago *Humans* took their first steps out of there and into the vast empty space, which was the earth then. But what has all this to do with Hugill and with us?'

A sudden silence fell. The music died away and the gorge was pervaded by an impenetrable secretive blackness. Then the dawn broke, an iridescent red and yellow sun nosed its way above the horizon, sending bold arrow-straight rays in a mad dash across sky and plain to fill the gorge with light, crags suddenly glowed orange and rock faces gleamed gold. At the very base of the gorge stood, alone, a magnificent baobab tree, it's peculiar up-ended branches reaching upwards, as if searching for roots not in the massive swollen trunk which sat uncomfortably on the earth, but in the very sky itself.

And beneath the tree, leaning against its pitted ancient bark, his beloved organ beside him, sat Hugill Macauley. A great sigh rose up amongst the animals as, one by one, they discerned his inert form, black against the irradiated tree.

CHAPTER TWENTY-TWO

HUGILL'S DISCOVERY

Kush shrieked and squawked with joy, his wings flapping wildly and his head jerking in and out. 'There he is! There he is! Come! Come!' he shouted, flying a little way over the gorge and exhorting us to get a move on with outstretched wings. The monkey slipped down the elephant's trunk with us and landed lightly on the plain. Then, without stopping, he leapt and bounded down the steep slope of the gorge. And Kush, dear Kush hovered impatiently above us, wanting to hurry and yet somehow afraid to go on alone.

We reached the base of the gorge. At long last I could see Hugill Macauley. He was sitting hunched over his legs, one long arm hanging limply at his side, the other curled inwards with elbow resting on knee and chin cupped in hand. As I got nearer still I saw that he was extremely old. His brown black fur, matted and worn thin in places, was fringed with white and he had a long scraggy grey flecked beard which hung in thin wisps below his chin. He was grinning widely at us, showing teeth that were yellow with age. Black wrinkles framed even blacker eyes, eyes, which seemed both young and old, sad and joyous by turns.

We were now within a few feet of where he sat. And then we noticed the bones! There were two piles of bones lying about three feet apart in front of him. They shone a luminous white in the dawn-light and looked dry, ageless, untouched as they must have been time out of mind. We looked at Hugill questioningly. He had a rather bemused expression on his face and was now stroking the back of his neck with the end of his tail.

Grandfather leapt to the ground and approached his old friend gently, paws outstretched: 'Hugill, you old wizard-prophet, my wise and good friend. Are you quite, quite well? How long we have searched for you and what hidden and wonderful things you have revealed to us. What great treasures! But what riddles you have woven around us too. And now I see there is another. For, what do all these bones mean?'

Hugill chuckled softly and suddenly did a somersault around the bones. Then he stopped before them and spoke in a light trickle of a voice: 'My friends, my unending quest throughout my long life has been to find my roots: The Origin of *my* Species, that place where they began to take their first simple and halting steps at the dawn of time. I thought that there, in my ancestral home, my own Eden, where the story of my people began, there I would be most myself; I would have a sense of belonging I have not had anywhere on earth. But I learned a strange thing as I went along. In this search for a beginning to my story, I found that the search itself was more important. For it was *Life*. And each step along the way has yielded small and exquisite treasures; treasures requiring careful and considered observation; treasures which have enlarged and expanded my visions and myself. More even than that! And this is the message to be told young Livingstone. I have found the greatest treasure of all: Continuity: that which underlies all things. You see, while the spirit of each life, that which one loves in each life, its essence, is remembered from generation to generation, there is no real beginning or ending to any life. The heart of each tale is passed on to the heart of the next tale, and so on…' and he stopped and beamed widely at us.

Grandfather hopped excitedly from one foot to the other. 'We have seen it! The spider's web, the snake, it was in the monkey's magic circle dance and the elephant's great burden of memory. Oh Hugill, it's all there, beneath everything. One just has to look for it.'

Hugill chuckled again. 'I knew you Darwin, of all creatures in this world would see it. But there is more. Still I pressed on with that one single aim. And now I have indeed found my ancestral beginnings. Right here in this gorge, very near to my Eden Garden (as I call it), the Great Forest. At first I thought that these bones,' and he gestured to one pile, 'belonged to my forebears, that in them lay the centre point of all my searches. I studied them in great detail in the light of all I have learned. But in the end they disappointed. They were somehow not quite as perfect as they should have been.' And he looked rather embarrassed as he said these words, perhaps even a little sad, as if there had been a great loss, that a grand mistake had been made. He continued, 'Of course, I soon realised that they belonged to rather an unsuccessful, distant branch on the family tree of primates and their heirs---*humans*---as we all know, have not generally lived up to expectations. They seem to have made so many mistakes in the ruling of this one and only planet of ours…this beautiful and bountiful earth.' He shook his head wistfully and picked up one of the bones and held it out. I leapt to the ground and crept over to him and examined the white bone. Then he threw it back on the pile, where it landed with a dry clunk.

He turned to the other pile of bones. 'Ahhh… but then I found these, right next to the others and these did not disappoint: for these were far more developed than the others and they did belong to my ancestors. Oh Darwin, Darwin, my old friend, don't you see what this means? It is a great discovery! It is the grandest of surprises!' He became quite breathless at this point and pulled us both close to his chest. I could feel his heart thudding fast against my cheek and sensed the excitement in the sharp exhales of breath on my whisker tips.

'You see this discovery has confirmed a growing suspicion I have had during all the many, many years I have travelled... from North to South and from East to West... about which branch is the true branch.' And as he said this, he looked up at the monkey leader and then at the whole troupe, which had by now joined us in the gorge. And they laughed and laughed and laughed, throwing their heads back and baring white teeth. When they finally stopped, I had the distinct feeling that, irrepressible creatures as they undoubtedly were, they had continued to share in this grand joke in that special blue-grey land of thought reserved for them.

Grandfather smiled. He leapt down again, reached forward and picked up one of the bones from the second pile. 'So, your last message then is to be found in these bones, that the Eden and the end lie here, that you monkeys are the true inheritors and not the other branch on the family tree at all... And this is why you have these special gifts denied *Humans* and this is what you stumbled on and wanted us to know... This is the story you want us to tell. Oh Hugill, how supremely clever! But there is more. There must be more! And I believe it lies in your grand discovery of Continuity. It must be the case that the lives to come will benefit from the special insights gained by the lives which have passed by, and so on and on, until in some distant time more will be understood and less mistakes will be made. That is your inheritance Hugill. That is the special burden you and your people must carry from generation to generation, on behalf of us all, including *Humans*, my friend.'

Kush began huffing loudly and blowing out his chest. He pushed his way roughly past Grandfather. 'Do you mean…do you mean that we have crossed a whole chunk of Africa, gone through untold dangers to get to you, to find these silly old bones? Nuts! I always said you were nuts! Bones! I ask you!'

'Oh Kush, my dearly beloved.' And Hugill stretched out a thin arm and Kush climbed onto it, venturing further until he had reached the old monkey's shoulder, whereupon he buried his yellow face in the dark fur. 'Alas yes...Kush is right of course, they are just bones in the end. And while you and I, Darwin, understand their significance, their discovery, as I said before, is not nearly as important as the great quest for them has been. That is the story to be told. It is the search for a beginning, which will be forever remembered and will never end. For in the search for a beginning we have found the Spirit of Continuity, that which unites us all down the centuries. As you so rightly suggest Darwin, the sense of belonging on earth lies there and not in the lessons of these bones.'

He looked up and smiled at Warrior, the Perceiver and then especially at the elephant, who trumpeted softly in response.

Were I to look into her eyes now, I'm sure I would see a strange collection of animals grouped beneath a baobab tree, beside an old organ and some funny white bones, there to lie forever alongside all the other events that made up our little journey. They would lie at a great distance from my gaze, as if they had already been swallowed up by time and had become yet another treasured moment in infinite memory, each one like fresh rainwater cupped in a green leaf.

Hugill gently lowered Kush and me to the ground and picked up his organ. He began to play a tune, the first his father had taught him, he said.

'What a cacophony! What a cacophony!' shrieked Kush, covering his ears with his wings.

Hugill chuckled and at the end of his tune, he put down his organ. And then, in a quiet voice, he whispered to Grandfather and me, 'How about stopping with me for a time in this forest?'

Grandfather looked at me and then turned to the monkey. 'There are a few things I still have to do in this imperfect world of ours Hugill my friend; just a few more things to find out and to show Livingstone. But may I consider it for the future?'

'Of course,' and he turned and looked amongst the animals. 'Perhaps we can persuade Warrior to fly you home. If you encouraged him to take frequent rests, the veriest hint of spring should be in the air by the time you arrived.'

With a great leap Hugill grabbed the bones, both human and monkey. He did three somersaults in the air and then lightly juggled all the bones. Higher and higher they went, the light catching them as they turned in the air before falling towards his outstretched hands.

And as I watched Hugill Macauley juggle those bones, it was as if they were joined together to form an unending chain going round and round, each one containing a little message---its own spirit---and passing it on to the next and the next… a pattern for life itself, all lives, time without end and time out of mind.

THE END

Or

THE BEGINNING